To: All witches, warlocks, sorcerers, wizards, fairies, garden gnomes, and other magic users

Sabrina glanced up. "There's such a thing as fairies? Cool!"

"Don't get distracted, dear," Zelda said. "Keep reading."

Re: Magic Blackout
The Witches' Council has received intelligence that Dr. Francisco Imperium, a mortal scientist connected with the Pentagon, will be conducting experiments to determine the existence of magic beginning today at 6:00 A.M. Witches' Standard Time. He is sending researchers to your area.

All magic users are hereby ordered to cease any use of magic for any reason, until Dr. Imperium leaves the area. You will be contacted when this ban is lifted.

Any questions or comments must be sent to the council before 6:00 A.M. After that time, there will be no contact between the Mortal Realm and the Other Realm until further notice.

Sabrina, the Teenage Witch™ books

Available from ARCHWAY Paperbacks

Sabrina the Teenage Witch™

Spying Eyes

Nancy Holder

AN ARCHWAY PAPERBACK
Published by POCKET BOOKS
New York London Toronto Sydney Tokyo Singapore

AN ARCHWAY PAPERBACK *Original*

An Archway Paperback published by
POCKET BOOKS, a division of Simon & Schuster Inc.
1230 Avenue of the Americas, New York, NY 10020

ISBN: 0-671-02118-4

First Archway Paperback printing September 1998

10 9 8 7 6 5 4 3 2 1

Printed in the U.S.A.

IL: 4+

For Tabitha and Tracey Van De Ven
and
Grace Elizabeth Hackett-Beck

and with sincere thanks to:
Lisa Clancy, Elizabeth Shiflett, Paul Ruditis,
Lindsay Sagnette, and Howard Morhaim

Spying Eyes

Chapter 1

☆

Bzzzzz.

Sabrina's alarm clock cut short what had been a very sweet dream that had something to do with Paris, a red Corvette convertible, and that hunky guy who manned the pretzel stand at the mall. Eager to return to the scene, Sabrina rolled over in the air three feet above her bed and pointed downward, aiming squarely at the clock on her nightstand, and muttered,

"Ten, nine, eight,
A few more zzzz's would be just great."

The clock obligingly stopped its loud and annoying *bzzzz* and switched to an even louder, more annoying *zzzzz.* Sabrina groaned and

opened one sleepy eye. All in the name of love—
and too many tardies in first period—her aunts
had conjured a fail-safe on the snooze button,
which Sabrina kept trying to thwart and which
so far had proved unthwartable. She couldn't
even get it to play music to awaken her, because
her aunts had discovered that Sabrina could
sleep through the most raucous rock, the thrash-
iest thrash, and heavy metal so heavy it weighed
twenty tons a note.

Opera, however, was another story, but she
wasn't about to let them know that.

Zzzzzz.

"All right, all right," she groaned, pulling her
pillow over her head to drown out the irritating
sound. "Relax. Stop noodging. I'm up."

Zzzzzz, the clock insisted. It was not easily
fooled.

Sabrina huffed and sat up. Immediately she
tumbled to the mattress.

Ooofff!

Salem the black cat, sleeping curled in a circle
at the foot of the bed, jerked as she crash-landed.
Half-awake, he muttered, "Lash the sails. There's
a storm. We'll attack with cutlasses and can-
nons." He blinked his big yellow eyes, looked
around, and sighed. "Darn," he muttered.

"Another shot at world domination shattered
by reality?" Sabrina asked, yawning. Salem was
actually a warlock who had been sentenced to
spend time as a feline as punishment for trying

to take over the mortal world. Sabrina's aunts had charge of him for the duration of his sentence.

"All I have left are my dreams," he said dramatically.

"*And* your days of doing nothing but eating and napping and watching lint float," Sabrina retorted. "Such a tough life."

"Oooh, I'm hearing math test in your day ahead." Salem stretched languidly, as if he hadn't a care in the world. Which aside from the usual feline concerns, he didn't. "And that we didn't study for it."

"Yes, well." She stepped into her slippers. It was true. This was not a day she was eager to begin. In all of last night's excitement hearing about Valerie's upcoming possible real live date with a possible real live guy who actually played in a band, Sabrina had, ah, sort of forgotten to study for today's math quiz. "I'll cram at breakfast. Or maybe I'll make a 'suggestion' to Mrs. Quick to forget about it, and—"

Salem shook his head. "Naughty, naughty, Sabrina. You've already gotten in trouble for using magic on your G.P.A., true?"

Sabrina grimaced. "I want to go back to bed."

Footsteps padded down the hallway—two sets of them—and paused outside Sabrina's bedroom door. "I can't believe she's still asleep," Sabrina's Aunt Hilda whispered. "Doesn't she know what day this is?"

"Actually, I don't think she does," her other aunt, Zelda, answered, also in a whisper. "Have we ever told her about Castanalia?"

Sabrina looked at Salem. "They haven't. What is it?"

Salem licked his forepaw. "It's nothing to do with *me,*" he said. "All *I* do these days is nap and watch lint float."

"Salem," Sabrina said sternly.

"And eat," he continued, ignoring her. "Don't forget eating. All *I* do is—"

The bedroom door burst open. "You're awake. Finally!" Hilda chirruped.

Sabrina stared. The shorter of her two aunts was swathed from head to toe in a strange, glowing fabric that continuously changed deep, vibrant color as she swept into the room. It looked like a neon sign in a blender set on puree. "I swear, Sabrina, you'd sleep through Halloween."

Zelda breezed in after Hilda. "No, she wouldn't. She just doesn't know what she's been missing."

Sabrina's eyes got bigger. Zelda's outfit featured a trim bodice, huge, puffy sleeves, and an enormous hoop skirt. The bodice was delicate gold lace, while the sleeves and skirt danced and glittered with golden sparkles that cast reflections on Sabrina's bedroom walls like a disco ball. Zelda was also wearing an immense tiara studded with diamonds—or, possibly, cubic zirconia, it was so hard to tell these days—and gold.

These were not her aunts' normal everyday clothes, not by half. Usually Hilda and Zelda Spellman dressed to blend into their small New England town of Westbridge—sweaters, skirts, or suits—not in the latest to-hex-for designer fashions from Witch-Mart. Especially Zelda, who as the older of the two sisters, felt it was her particular responsibility to set a good example for Sabrina in all departments, including what to don for witch's camouflage as she moved among mortals and pretended to be one of them.

"Good morning, Glinda One and Glinda Two," Sabrina teased, referring to the Good Witch in *The Wizard of Oz*. As a matter of fact, Zelda's costume was very similar to Glinda's. "What's Catsanalia?"

"Okay, I give. It's when all the cats in the known universe go on tour," Salem said. "Their legions of adoring slaves—I mean, fans—throw them catnip and tuna fish. Shower them with riches. Feed them grapes. Give them pedicures." He grunted and said, "Don't mind me. I'm not bitter. Just nostalgic for the old days."

"*Cast*analia," Zelda said. "C-A-S-T. Not *Cats*-analia. It has nothing to do with cats." She slid a sidelong glance at Salem. "Or *bitter* ex-warlocks."

"Temporarily ex. Semipermanently bitter," Salem interjected.

"And?" Sabrina prodded. "Is it like the Grammys? Do I need a hot outfit, too?" She certainly hoped so.

Hilda plopped excitedly on the bed and spread her arms. Her gown danced and shimmered as wave after wave of blue and green crashed across the skirt.

Salem murmured, "That dress is making me seasick. Cat overboard," and jumped down to the floor.

"You can have a fancy dress if you want. You can have anything you want!" Hilda exclaimed, smiling broadly. "Castanalia is the best day of the year for those of us who live in the mortal world."

"It is?" Sabrina asked, catching her excitement. "Does it involve presents?" *Or skipping math?*

"It's the best day of the year for those of us who are *witches* who live in the mortal world," Zelda said. She snapped her fingers. Her outfit immediately became more Aunt Zelda-ish: an elegant pearl gray sweater and a black skirt that brushed the tops of her knees. She looked like an attractive, brainy scientist off to deliver a physics lecture, which was usually a good guess if you had to figure out where Zelda was.

She went on, "Sabrina, Castanalia is also called 'All-You-Can-Cast Day.' You can use magic to your heart's content from now until midnight. You can do any witchy thing you want!"

Sabrina raised her eyebrows as she studied their shiny, eager faces. They reminded her of two excited mortal kids about to rip into their Christmas presents. "But I'm always getting in trouble for using my magic. I mean, using it at the wrong time or the wrong place," she amended, thinking of several dozen times she had learned the hard way which times and places those were.

When you had magic powers, it was hard not to point and conjure whenever you wanted. However, there were consequences—sometimes dire ones—to abusing such powers. Salem, doomed to be a cat for misusing his magical abilities, was the unspoken lesson in her house. Being a witch was very complicated. So complicated that if life was fair, she ought to get extra credit for it at school.

"Well, you won't get in trouble for using magic today," Hilda cheerily assured her. "Because today doesn't really exist."

"That's right," Zelda agreed. "You see, Sabrina, the Witches' Council instituted All-You-Can-Cast Day once every few years so that those of us witches who live in the mortal realm can let off a little steam. We can work all the spells we wish because at midnight, they all undo. Oh, except for . . ."

She trailed off as thunder rumbled in the

distance, followed by a crash of lightning. "Someone's coming through the closet," she said, referring to their linen closet, which served as a portal to the Other Realm. "Hilda, tell her the rest."

"It might be one of my adoring fans," Salem said hopefully, following Zelda out the door. He turned and said over his shoulder, "Hey, it could happen."

Sabrina and Hilda traded glances. "We didn't say anything to the contrary," Hilda said.

Sabrina giggled. Hilda pointed the door shut and took Sabrina's hands in hers. Aunt Hilda was shorter than Zelda, and when she smiled, her grin more mischievous. She, more often than Zelda, initiated the high jinks around their house. She was the one who showed Sabrina how to cook up some Man Brew on the Lab-Top. And it was she who decided she and Zelda should turn into teenagers so they could accompany Sabrina and her friends on their trip to Boston to meet the Violent Femmes.

Sabrina remembered when she had first come to live with her aunts. Her parents had divorced, and her archeologist mother had flown off to Peru to dig for artifacts. Because he was supposedly in the foreign service, Sabrina's father had always traveled a lot. The official explanation given to Sabrina was that because of her parents' far-flung interests, Hilda and Zelda would see to providing her with a stable home while she finished high school.

Little did Sabrina realize that on the morning of her sixteenth birthday, she would wake up levitating above her bed. And her aunts would reveal themselves as witches, and tell her that she herself was half-mortal and half-witch. It turned out that her father was in the *very* foreign service. He was a warlock she could talk to in her book of magic if she needed to. And if she saw her mother, who was a mortal, during the next two years, Mom would turn into a ball of wax. It was a rule instituted by the Witches' Council to discourage mixed marriages between mortals and witches.

Talk about your non-nuclear family!

"So. I can use all the magic I want?" Sabrina asked, coming back to the matter at hand.

"Absolutely. You can make yourself queen for a day. Or Harvest Dance princess," Hilda added slyly, apparently remembering that Westbridge High's big dance was coming up. And remembering, too, that Sabrina had confided a shy little wish that it would be awfully nice to be voted onto the Harvest Dance court. . . .

"What's the catch?" Sabrina had discovered that where magic was involved, there generally was one. That was why witches had to study their handbooks and get their learner's permits before moving on to receiving licenses to zap.

Just then Zelda walked back in loaded with a pile of books and a clipboard.

"Hilda, it's our selections for the Witches' Book of the Month Club." Grunting, she set down the pile and picked the first book off the top. It was an enormous thing with a boring brown cover. "What do you think? *Theoretical Axioms and Magical Applications of Quantum Physics.* It looks fascinating."

As Sabrina and Hilda hid their grins, Zelda paged eagerly through it. "And it's just loaded with footnotes!" she said happily. "Or how about this?" She showed them the cover of the second one. There was a drawing of a paw embossed in gold and in big three-dimensional letters, the title *Women Who Turn into Wolves.*

Hilda wrinkled her nose. "Don't they have any trashy Hollywood novels?"

"Yes, I think so," Zelda replied. She checked the clipboard. "Yes. According to the order sheet, there's something called *Rodeo Dive Shop.* It's supposed to be a lot like *Baywatch.* Only with scantier bathing suits and deeper tans."

Hilda clapped her hands. "That sounds good."

"Well, then here." Zelda lifted up the next book and examined the cover. And the next. And the next. She frowned as she went through the stack. "It seems to be missing."

"You can have it when I'm done," Salem called from another part of the house. "I'm already on chapter two."

"Actually, this can wait," Zelda said, putting down the clipboard. She beamed at her niece. "After all, we don't want to waste a moment of Sabrina's first Castanalia!"

"No, indeedy!" Hilda agreed. She pointed at Sabrina, who was instantly dressed in her favorite velvet jeans and short-sleeve sweater. Then she snapped her fingers and the three of them were seated at the breakfast table in the kitchen of their Victorian house. Happy-face pancakes grinned up at Sabrina. Oranges bobbed in the air and squeezed themselves into her glass.

Sabrina stared down at the pancakes, picked up her fork, then put it back down again. She said, "This is cool, but I'm not really hungry."

"Not hungry?" Zelda asked. She leaned forward and felt Sabrina's forehead. "You're not sick, are you, dear? Hilda, get the spellfluenza bottle out of the cabinet."

Hilda also laid her palm over Sabrina's forehead. She touched her cheek for good measure. "Zelda, she's as cool as a cucumber. You're such a worrywart."

Hilda cut into her pancake, which said, "Have a nice day."

"Thank you," Hilda replied, and popped it into her mouth. "They're very delicious, Sabrina. And courteous, too."

Sabrina shook her head. "I'm not sick. I guess I'm just a little nervous. I'm not used to casting all the spells I want."

"Oh, sweetie, it's just like riding a skateboard," Hilda offered, patting her niece's arm. Sometime in the last five seconds, she had abandoned her kaleidoscopic gown and changed into a big green pullover and black leggings.

"I've never ridden a skateboard," Sabrina confessed.

"What?" Hilda cried. "Well, there's no time like the present."

Before Sabrina knew what was happening, she was perched on a skateboard barreling down the street at about fifty miles an hour.

Like an echo off a mountain, she heard Zelda say, "The term is 'just like riding a bicycle,' Hilda. Not a skateboard."

"Oh, you're right," Hilda said. "Sorry."

"I'm not sorry!" Sabrina cried. "Whoo-hoo!" The wind whipped her hair as she shot down a small hill. This was really exciting!

So far, All-You-Can-Cast Day was a fun fest. Imagine, casting a spell for anything you ever wanted! And you didn't have to be careful, because everything automatically changed back at midnight.

"Time to go for the gold!" she shouted, flicking her wrist. Soon she was clocking sixty, then seventy, then pretty darn close to breaking the sound barrier. "Faster!" she cried. "Magic mania, here I come!"

Once she got to school, she'd let out all the stops. She'd share her day with all her friends by fulfilling their dreams for one short day.

Hey, what could possibly go wrong?

☆

Chapter 2

☆

Sabrina went so fast on her skateboard that she broke the time barrier and arrived at school an hour early. "Cool!" she cried, as she stood before the two-story redbrick building with the squared-off slanted roofs that reminded her aunts of their days in eighteenth-century Amsterdam. Supertemporal skateboarding was a much better way to avoid tardies than trying to outwit an obsessed alarm clock.

She looked around, not sure what to do with an extra preschool hour. For a moment she wondered if she was allowed to speed up time during Castanalia. In her admittedly limited experience, time and witchcraft were not usually two elements that mixed well. When she had just arrived in Westbridge and made a mess of her first day at school, it had taken a special petition to the Witches' Council to relive those twenty-four hours so she could have another chance at dating, popularity, and decent grades. Sabrina suspected her petition had been granted only because the then-leader of the Witches' Council, Drell, used to date her Aunt Hilda. One could only call in a favor like that so often. Like maybe once.

Besides, there was a math quiz from last week with her name on it—and a big red C next to the doodle of a very unhappy face and the words *Sabrina, see me after class.* An hour of study might not change that C into an A, but it could at least make it a B-plus.

"What am I thinking?" she asked, smacking her forehead. "I *can* change that C into an A with a flick of my wrist." *But just for today,* she realized. Today would happen all over again tomorrow, and that C would go back on her permanent record.

Still, it would be fun. She pointed her finger at herself and chanted:

> *"Hey, hey, hey,*
> *Today in math I get an A!"*

"Sabrina?" someone said behind her.

Startled, Sabrina jumped, lost her balance, and toppled off the skateboard onto her behind. Harvey Kinkle, one of her favorite mortals, hurried over to her.

"Gee, did you hurt yourself?" he asked. He reached down to help her up. He wore a Fighting Scallions sweatshirt and a pair of sweatpants that looked good with his athletic build, light brown hair, and hazel eyes. The Scallions was the name of Westbridge High's athletic teams. It was supposed to have been Stallions, but a printer had made an error, and the school decided to keep the name. The adults thought it was nice to have something that was a little different. And the kids had gotten used to all the teasing from the other schools.

For the most part.

"No, I'm not hurt," she fibbed. She smiled up at him and took his hand. "When you surf the pavement, you have to be ready for a pretty dramatic wipeout now and then."

"I didn't know you skateboarded," he said, looking impressed There was a soft sheen of moisture on his forehead, and he was panting slightly, as if he'd been running.

"Oh, sure. I like to keep my hand in. Or my feet on." She indicated his workout clothes. "What about you?"

"I'm trying to get in shape for the game this Friday." This Friday was the first game of the Scallions' football season. It was all anyone at school was talking about. That and the upcoming Harvest Dance, and who would be crowned king and queen. "I'm hoping to start. Of course, I'm always hoping to start." He looked both excited and nervous. Kind of the way Salem looked whenever the linen closet boomed.

"I'm sure you will," she assured him. She always supported him. And he was always warming the bench.

"Yeah, well." He looked down at her skateboard. "That's a cool piece of fiberglass. But you know, we're not allowed to bring skateboards or in-lines to school. If Mr. Kraft sees it, he'll impound it."

"Not today he won't," she said, grinning. "Hey, Harvey, hop on. Take a ride on the wild side."

Harvey looked tempted. He glanced left, then right. "I don't know. I can't get in trouble for anything until after Friday. If I got benched, my dad would kill me." Harvey had a teeny timid side that sometimes landed him in awkward predicaments. He was more likely to go along with the crowd than someone might guess on first meeting him. But that was part of his good, easygoing nature, and Sabrina loved that about him.

"You won't get in trouble," she said. "I promise."

He shrugged as he considered. It was obvious he was dying to try it out. "I dunno."

"Go ahead," she urged. "There's no one here but us daredevils. Not even Mr. Kraft will show up for school this early."

"Well, okay." As she knew he would, he gave

in. He stepped on, getting the feel of it, and then he pressed the ball of his right foot against the ground.

She pointed her finger and said to the board:

> *"Harvey is my fearless friend.*
> *Make him ride just like the wind!"*

Harvey took off in a blur. The board accelerated, the wheels whirring so fast they began to smoke. Sabrina laughed and waved as he jetted past her.

Then the board popped a wheelie and Harvey shouted, "How do you stooooooop this thing?"

"Like this," she answered, pointing quickly. Then she gritted her teeth and said, "Whoops," as the board screeched to a stop and Harvey hurtled through the air like a human cannon ball.

"Heeeeeelp!" he cried, his arms and legs flailing as he soared through the sky.

Sabrina started to panic. What spell should she use to cushion his fall? She pointed at Harvey and said:

> *"Don't laugh or gloat,*
> *Look at Harvey float!"*

Immediately he stopped falling. "Sabrina, look! I'm saved!" he called down to her from about twenty feet above the ground. Then his expression of intense relief transformed to one of shock. "Oh, my gosh, I'm hanging in the air!"

For a split second Sabrina was overcome with the distinct feeling that she had just committed the witches' equivalent of a major felony. Mortals were not supposed to know a) that she was half witch, or b) that witches and magic existed at all. But today didn't exist, right? She could do whatever she wanted.

Right!

Happily, she pointed him down to earth, where he landed on his feet with a gentle thud.

"Drastic!" he cried. "Wow, Sabrina, a turbo-charged, radio-controlled skateboard. It's really cool," Harvey enthused. "I want to go again. Where on earth did you buy that thing?"

"Nowhere on Earth," she said, chuckling, beckoning the skateboard toward them. It zoomed up and flipped onto its end as if standing at attention. Maybe she should introduce it to her obedient little alarm clock.

Just then the bell rang. Had an entire hour really flown by?

"Let's ride some some more after school," Harvey suggested. "And I want to go to that store you mentioned and get my own."

Sabrina paused, confused. "That other store?"

"Yeah, what did you call it? Nowhere on Earth. Wow, you've got to show me the control mechanism." He squatted down. "I can't figure out how I floated down."

"It's a special feature." She giggled. *Magic.*

"Well, it's very cool. Listen," he added, "I've got to grab a shower before class."

"Okay. See you later." Sabrina smiled and gave him a wave.

They went their separate ways. Next item on Sabrina's magical agenda was a killer new outfit. In fact, she decided she would create a new one for each class period. Then she'd give every Westbridge student who had ever done something nice thing for her, Harvey, or Valerie A's in all their classes.

Planning her day's wardrobe, Sabrina headed for the girls' room for her first costume change. The corridor walls were covered with posters urging the students to vote for various seniors for the Harvest Dance royal court. There would be a king and queen from the senior class, and then a princess and escort from the junior and sophomore classes. Sabrina sighed. She just knew she would never be nominated for something like that, even if her aunts insisted she had just as good a chance as anyone else.

She pushed open the door, only to find Valerie standing before the mirror with a tube of lipstick in her hand.

Valerie was her best friend, and she wanted like anything to be one of the cool kids. She was sweet and cute, with dark brown hair and matching eyes, and she and Sabrina spent a lot of time together, doing the things best friends do—

talking about their dreams, their frustrations, and boys.

Valerie saw Sabrina's reflection and smiled at her as she whirled around. Her dark eyes flashed, and she was smiling like she'd won the lottery. "Sabrina, hi. Guess what! Brian Enders said he wanted to talk to me before first period. I'm *soooo* nervous. Maybe he's going to ask me out!"

"Great, Valerie!" Sabrina clapped her hands. Brian Enders was one of the most popular boys in school. He had a garage band called Gruff Baby that had actually played a couple of gigs in local teen clubs. If he took Valerie out on a date, she would probably be accepted by the other popular kids as one of them.

"Or maybe it's not to ask me out," Valerie worried, touching her lips with her fingernail. "Remember that time Chris Silver asked me to sit next to him in the movies?"

Sabrina made a face. She knew it had been one of the most humiliating episodes in Valerie's life. It turned out Chris had only asked Valerie to sit down in order to save his and his best friend's seats while they stood in line for popcorn. When they'd come back, Chris asked Valerie to move, and she hadn't been able to find a seat for herself in the crowded theater.

Until Sabrina sort of "found" one for her.

Meanwhile, the lid on Chris's drink had "sort of" come unsnapped. When he unknowingly took a big swig of root beer, it cascaded down his shirt and soaked his jeans. He had had to leave ten minutes into the feature presentation.

"Why wouldn't Brian ask you out?" Sabrina said loyally. The truth was, Valerie lacked a little something in the self-esteem department. Sometimes—okay, truth, lots of times—she scared boys off without realizing it because she was so grateful for their attention and overly eager for their approval.

Sabrina thought about suggesting to Valerie that she reapply her lipstick. In her nervous state Valerie had chewed it all off. Then Sabrina remembered what day it was. Pointing when Valerie wasn't looking, she touched it up. She also gave her a little more blush. Arched her brows.

Meddle, meddle, meddle.

"Well . . ." Sabrina said gently, pushing open the bathroom door.

As Valerie followed Sabrina out, she put her hands around her own neck. "Why do I feel like I'm walking to my own execution?"

"You're not used to cool guys asking you out," Sabrina offered helpfully. She grinned. "But get used to it, okay?"

"Who's asking who out?" Libby Chessler, Westbridge High's answer to a soap opera queen, strolled up and put a nicely manicured hand on Valerie's shoulder. Her two equally shallow girl-friends, Cee Cee and Jill, came up on either side of Libby and struck poses like they were vogueing in a rock video. Only really popular girls could do things like that and not be laughed right out of school.

"A question was posed!" Libby said imperiously.

"Uh, n-no one," Valerie stammered, glancing anxiously at Sabrina. Sabrina got the message loud and clear: *Don't say a word.* Libby was such an expert at bursting balloons that Sabrina suspected she carried a box of pushpins in her purse.

"That's what I figured," Libby said. "No one." She gave her short cheerleader skirt a twirl, as if to remind Valerie and Sabrina that in the pecking order of school popularity, cheerleaders were cool. Sabrina and Valerie were not.

"Who would go out with a nerd or a freak?" Libby asked sweetly. She loved to call them that, and did so at every opportunity. Sabrina figured that as a witch, maybe she herself did qualify for freakhood, but it still hurt each time Libby said it. And it made her mad when she saw her own hurt feelings reflected in Valerie's eyes. Sabrina had a whole other life with her witchy relatives—skiing on Mars, going to dinner parties in the Other Realm (even if her little terror of a cousin, Amanda, was at them), and riding her vacuum cleaner by the light of the moon. But mortal high school life was all Valerie had.

Sabrina was just about to say—or more important, do—something—when the cheerleader looked past them, stood up a little straighter, and waved at someone behind them.

"Oh, hi, Brian!" Libby called in a sickeningly sweet singsong.

Sure enough, big, blond, handsome Brian Enders waved and strode down the corridor. He wore black jeans and a very cool black leather jacket.

Valerie whispered, "Oh, no, Sabrina, I can't talk to him now. Libby's here and she's going to ruin everything!" Nervously she twisted her fingers as she pulled her books tightly against her chest.

Before Sabrina could respond, Brian reached them. He put an arm around Libby and smiled broadly at her. Then he turned to Valerie and said, "Oh, hey. Here you are."

"Yes," Valerie said breathlessly. "I are here. I am," she corrected. "Here."

"Good. Listen, it's about my band."

"Yes?" Valerie said even more breathlessly. Her cheeks were turning pink. Surreptitiously Sabrina nodded in encouragement. Valerie didn't need her help. Something magical was going to happen to her naturally!

Brian said, "We need a lead singer."

"Yes?" Valerie squeaked.

"And Libby said she'd love to do it, but she needs someone to walk her dog after school. I told her, 'Valerie never has anything to do after school. Ask her.' But she figured you'd feel pressured to say yes, her being a cheerleader and all."

"Bri-an," Libby said, rolling her eyes and smiling, as if pretending to be embarrassed. Which she was not at all, not one bit. In fact, the arrows she shot Valerie as she kept the smile frozen in place would have dropped a mastodon.

"But you'll do it, right, Val?" Brian asked with a smile that would have done any politician proud.

"Oh," Valerie said in a tiny voice.

Sabrina gritted her teeth. Valerie had probably imagined Brian smiling just this smile a million times, asking her to go to the Slicery or maybe even catch a movie, seated side by side, not twenty-one rows away from each other as it had been with her and Chris. Sabrina guessed that never in those one million times had Valerie included his asking her to walk some other girl's dog.

Brian touched Valerie's hand, cocked his head, and smiled helplessly. "I'd consider it such a great favor. He's a very cool dog. His name is Abdul—"

"For Paula Abdul," Libby cut in. "She got her start as a cheerleader." She smiled at Valerie. "Won't you help me? I'll let all the other girls on the squad know what a great sport you are."

Valerie's eyes began to well up with tears. "Oh." She blinked hard. "Sure."

"See, Libby? I told you she'd jump at the chance to help you." Brian clapped Valerie on the shoulder with his free hand, then laced his fingers through Libby's and swung her arm. "Come on, Lib, we'll be late for class."

"I'll pay you," Libby said over her shoulder to Valerie. "Does a dollar an hour sound fair?"

Valerie sniffled. As soon as Libby and Brian were out of earshot, she turned to Sabrina and swallowed hard. "I'd start crying, but the tardy bell's going to ring," she said miserably. "And if I'm late one more time, I'll get detention. And I am not going to cry in detention again. I'm getting a very lousy reputation in there."

"Oh, Valerie," Sabrina said. "I'm so sorry."

"If I was dating a rock musician, I'd finally have some status in this school. I guess I'm doomed to geekhood, Sabrina. Just like Libby says." Valerie held out her wrists like a prisoner. "Just sign me up for nerd patrol. Lead the way to the audiovisual equipment so I can operate it for health class."

Val was giving up. Giving *in* to Libby's opinion of her. Sabrina could see it in her eyes.

And she knew exactly what to do.

"No way, Valerie. You're going to be the most popular girl in school yet!" Sabrina said. She pointed.

Valerie disappeared.

At once, kids came running down the hall, parting around Sabrina like buffalo on a stampede. They were cheering and gesturing toward the entrance to the school. Someone cried, "Who's got a camera?"

Someone else shouted, "They're pulling up!"

Breathless, Libby ran into Sabrina. "I'm sorry," she said sweetly, then looked envious. "Gosh, Sabrina, you're Valerie's best friend. You're so lucky."

"Yeah," said Brian Enders, catching up with Libby. "Come on, Lib. Maybe she'll give us her autograph."

The kids flocked outside. A long stretch limo hugged the curb. The windows were tinted. Three burly men in jeans and black satin jackets that read VALERIE ROAD TOUR scanned the crowd through wraparound sunglasses.

"Those are her bodyguards, aren't they?" Libby shouted in Sabrina's ear as the crowd began cheering. One of the limo's passenger doors was opening.

First, a man in a jeweled jumpsuit and a cape climbed out. He wore sunglasses and kept his head down. Everyone cheered and waved at him. He murmured, "Thank you, thank you very much."

Then Valerie appeared, in wide bell-bottoms, a spaghetti-strap shirt, and fat-soled tennis shoes. The tattoo on her arm was a red rose shaped to resemble a musical note.

"Hey," she said to everyone, and they went completely crazy. They tried to push their way past her bodyguards as the limo pulled away from the curb.

Libby jumped up and down and clapped her hands. "Valerie, we love you!" she said. Tears of joy streamed down her cheeks. "Oh, I can't believe she's come back to Westbridge," she gushed, grabbing on to Brian.

"If only she'd asked me to play in her band," Brian replied. "I'd be on the road with my bass." He sighed. "But I know I'm not good enough for her."

Libby patted him sympathetically. "Just keep practicing, Brian," she urged. "Maybe someday you'll hit the big time, too."

Valerie's bodyguards parted the kids as Valerie and her mystery companion moved toward the entrance of the school, where Mr. Kraft was waiting for them with open arms.

"Elvis, I knew you weren't dead!" he cried. "I've saved all your records! I still even have a bottle of Love Me Tender shampoo."

The man in the cape and the sunglasses murmured, "Thank you. Thank you very much." He saw Sabrina and waved at her. "Hey, little yellow-headed gal. How you doin'?"

Sabrina grinned This was so cool! *Wait till Harvey sees this guy!* "I think my work here is finished," she said to herself. She made a show of wiping her hands, then pointed and disappeared. Her disembodied voice added, "So many spells. So little time."

Sabrina felt this was a school. Normal weird says, but she really? "I don't know, says Sabrina, and he said to be sad. She said a show of concern in class, from normal mode, he said the description and says, under. So doing such...

Chapter 3

☆

☆

School was fun when you could control it. All day long Sabrina cast spell after spell, including changing the cafeteria food into pizza direct from the Slicery and making Vice-principal Kraft the education adviser to the President of the United States.

Not so much for revenge but for the sheer fun of it, Sabrina turned Libby back into the nerd Sabrina had once made her, the nerd who was the president of the science club and loving it. Libby's usually very stylish dark hair was pulled back into a bun and she wore very thick glasses that might have been trendy if the rest of Libby's look said "retro." But the rest of Libby's look only said, "Don't look."

But that was okay; according to Sabrina's spell, Libby was the kind of nerd who took pride in ignoring the superficial dictates of taste and style. As were her science club vice-president and secretary, Jill and Cee Cee.

On the other hand, Sabrina was heavily immersed in the superficial dictates of taste and fashion. She quickly discovered that yellow was not her color but chocolate brown most definitely was, especially if it involved tight and stretchy pants. She also learned that Valerie the famous rock star looked excellent in red sequins, and Harvey, well, Sabrina thought he looked pretty neat in just about anything. Sweats. Jeans. A tux. A carrot suit.

Suddenly all the school calendars had everyone convinced it was Friday (another way of getting around the pesky time issue), and they were all magically transported to the Scallions' stadium for the first game of the season. Thanks to a lot of fancy pointing—and invisible sunglasses, which made everyone think it was night—no one thought a thing of it.

Of course, Harvey was in the starting lineup.

"He's amazing!" the man seated beside Sabrina said. "I'm a scout from Boston University, and I think that boy's got what we want."

"He'll be like this all season," Sabrina told him, having fun with the fantasy.

"How are his grades?"

"Straight A's," Sabrina said proudly. That had been an inspired spell, if she did say so herself.

"He'll be hearing from us, " said the scout.

At halftime Valerie and her mysterious friend who looked exactly like Elvis gave a free concert on a stage erected in the middle of the football field, starting off with "Heartbreak Hotel." Valerie insisted that Sabrina play with the band and handed her a tambourine. While Valerie belted out the blues, Sabrina rocked out on the stage as the lighted text display of a blimp cruising overhead read WESTBRIDGE LOVES YOU, VALERIE.

"Thank you, thank you," Valerie panted into the mike after a few songs. "I owe all this to my best friend, Sabrina Spellman, who never, ever stopped believing in me."

"Well, what are best friends for?" Sabrina asked.

"And Sabrina, I hope you never, ever stop believing in yourself," Valerie added over the P.A. system. "Now, listen to this, Westbridge!" The band played a chord. "I present to you Sabrina, your Harvest Queen!"

Suddenly Sabrina was wearing a long white formal dress. A red velvet cape was draped over her shoulders, and she carried a huge bouquet of at least three dozen roses.

She blinked. She hadn't conjured up a spell for any of this! Then she saw Aunt Hilda waving to her from the bleachers. Sabrina laughed and waved back. What a nice gift for Castanalia. It made her feel good to know that her aunts listened to her tales of woe about her lack of school popularity. She pointed at Hilda in return and winked at her.

"And I give you Harvey, your Harvest King!" Valerie shouted.

"Cool!" Harvey cried from the field. He wore his football uniform. Still sweaty from the game, he charged down the fifty-yard line with a large, sparkling crown under his arm. He vaulted onto the stage and placed the crown on Sabrina's head.

Her Supreme Nerdness Libby and her two nerdy friends, Cee Cee and Jill, made up Sabrina's court. Libby carried the train of Sabrina's robe, all the while murmuring facts about the periodic table of the elements to herself.

"This is so cool. It's too bad none of it is real," Sabrina murmured as she waved to the cheering crowds.

Harvey, standing beside her, whispered, "I know it's hard to believe, but it *is* real. You've got to believe that dreams can come true."

Mr. Kraft, looking very pompous—make that important—crossed the stage and took the mike. It whined with feedback. He clapped his hands.

"Attention, please! It's my great pleasure to announce the winner of the award for the Scallions' most valuable player of all time! And as the new education adviser to the President of the United States, it is my distinct pleasure to introduce to you that very President, who will present the award." He beamed. "Our President, Hilda Spellman!"

"Whoo-hoo!" Sabrina yelled, applauding with the rest of the crowd.

Hilda was *poofed!* onto the stage. She wore a nicely tailored black suit and an enormous brooch with the presidential seal in diamonds, rubies, and sapphires. A guy near the foot of the stage murmured, "Wow, check out the Prez!"

Harvey looked confused. "Sabrina," he said, "your aunt's the President? Since when?"

"Since the last election," she said, pointing at him to make him "remember."

"Oh, yeah." He laughed. "How could I have forgotten a thing like that?"

"Welcome, Madam President," Mr. Kraft began, then cleared his throat and smiled at the crowd. "If you'll excuse me, I've prepared a few remarks to welcome our esteemed guest." He reached into the breast pocket of his suit and pulled out a piece of paper. As he shook it out, it unrolled like a scroll all the way down to the floor.

"Well, this will take a while," Aunt Hilda whispered to Sabrina as she sidled over to her. Harvey was listening raptly to Mr. Kraft.

"You should hear him make the morning announcements over the P.A. system," Sabrina told her. "You can get an entire essay written."

She flushed. "I mean, if you hadn't done it the night before, like you should have."

"Long-windedness does have its upsides," Hilda agreed, allowing Sabrina's remark about not doing her homework to fly away like a little fruit bat. She grinned. "So far, being the President is fun. Everyone always assumes Zelda's the smart, in-charge one and I'm, well, modesty forbids me to go on, but, hey, the fun, cute one."

Sabrina nodded. "But you're also the leader of the free world."

"Indeed I am." Hilda rubbed her hands together. "Why, I could start World War III with one phone call if I wanted! Not that I want to," she added quickly. "It's just that it's fun to contemplate. Well, not exactly *fun . . .*"

"I know what you mean, Aunt Hilda," Sabrina told her. "It's exciting to get to do all the things we usually can't do in the mortal realm."

"Exactly. It's like a witch-wide version of teenage rebellion." She touched Sabrina's arm. "Not that we've had any trouble with you, dear."

"Thank you, Aunt Hilda." She gestured to her dress. "And thank you for making me Harvest Queen. You know it'll never happen in real life."

Hilda wagged a finger at her. "Sabrina, don't be so down on yourself."

"And as I look over my life as an educator," Mr. Kraft was droning on, "I can say it was in the sixties that I began to realize that the privileges of academic life do not excuse one from the other weighty responsibilities of society."

"I think that's his way of saying he participated in a lot of sit-ins," Hilda whispered. "He was quite the militant radical hippie-type."

"No way," Sabrina said, taking another look at the prim, button-down man.

"Way. Big way," Hilda assured her. "I just looked up his record. Oh, the things I could tell you, Sabrina—"

"May I present to you the President of the United States, Hilda Spellman!" Mr. Kraft finished up.

"My cue, at last," Hilda said. She raised her chin and threw back her shoulders as the crowd applauded.

Hilda began. "It is my distinct pleasure as the leader of the free world to honor an outstanding American mortal, I mean person. Well, he's not so much a person as a guy." She grimaced and glanced over at Sabrina, then shrugged and pointed. Immediately words began traveling across Hilda's field of view on an invisible levitating TelePrompTer, and she read the words as they appeared.

"And so, my fellow Americans," she said smoothly, "it's my distinct pleasure to present this trophy to the most valuable Scallion running back of all time!"

It was Sabrina's turn to point. A three-foot-tall trophy topped by a running football player materialized in Mr. Kraft's arms. Surprised, he staggered a little under the weight.

"I'd like the recipient of this trophy to come forward at this time," Hilda announced. "Harvey Kinkle!"

"Yay, Harvey!" Sabrina cried, clapping her hands.

Harvey looked pleased and amazed. He gave her hand a squeeze and said, "Be right back."

He crossed the stage as Valerie's band thrashed a few bars of "Born to Be Wild." Mr. Kraft staggered toward him and thrust the trophy into his arms.

Harvey cleared his throat and said, "Wow. Harvest King and MVP. This has to be one of the most amazing days of my life."

"Oh, I just love meddling in mortal affairs," Hilda said to Sabrina as she returned to the side of the stage. "You know, Zelda and I had gotten stuck in a bit of a rut in the way we celebrated Castanalia. It's so much fun to have a new witch around to add some spice." She looked around. "Do you want me to push the dance up to now?"

Sabrina shrugged. "Naw. I think it's time to do something else."

"Good. I want to go home and get Zelda. Then we'll really go nuts!"

Harvey grunted as he carried his trophy to Sabrina and nearly dropped it on her toe.

"Look, Sabrina. Isn't it cool?"

"Very, very cool, Harvey. I'm so happy for

you." Giving him the trophy wasn't at all like when she cheated at the martial arts tournament and won her trophy with magic. As Hilda pointed out, this was all for fun.

While Harvey set down the trophy, Hilda pointed upward. Instantly a large vacuum cleaner began to descend toward the stage. Emblazoned on the side was VACUUM FORCE ONE.

"Whoa! Look up in the sky!" Harvey cried.

"It's a bird," Jill said.

"It's a plane," Cee Cee insisted.

"It's a vacuum cleaner!" Valerie proclaimed with a riff on her guitar. Her band picked up the semimelodic line and went berserk on their instruments for about ten seconds.

"The melting point of neon is two hundred forty-eight point six degrees Celsius," Libby said.

Sabrina stood on tiptoe and gave Harvey a peck on the cheek. "That's our ride," she said to him. "Gotta go!"

As the entire stadium watched in awestruck silence, the Harvest Queen and the President of the United States hopped onto the vacuum cleaner and blasted up, up, and away.

☆

Chapter 4

☆

Zelda! We're home!" Hilda called as the vacuum cleaner whooshed through the back door and deposited Sabrina and President Spellman in the kitchen.

"Oh, good. The president of Russia called," Salem said from the countertop. "He wants you two to have a summit in a country whose main industry is fishing."

"Oh?" Hilda asked. "Which one?"

"He didn't specify." Salem looked intrigued. "How many are there, and could you please transport me to each one in order of amount of fish caught?" He blinked his big yellow eyes at her. "Pretty please? For All-You-Can-Cast Day?"

"Salem, don't you want to come with us?"

Zelda asked as she breezed into the kitchen. She was wearing a leather bomber jacket, aviator's goggles, and a long white silk scarf looped several times around her neck. "Hello, Your Majesty. Madam President," she said, chuckling as she pulled on a fleece-lined pair of leather gloves. "Well, I'm ready."

Sabrina looked from one aunt to the other. "Ready for what, joining an air show?" She eyed Hilda suspiciously. "Did you change your mind about that phone call?"

Zelda looked at Hilda. "What's she talking about?"

Hilda shrugged. "Never mind. Sabrina, while we were flying home, I sent a thoughtgram to Zelda and told her how much fun I'm having with you. We decided to ask you to lead us on a tour of the universe!" She pointed at Sabrina, who was instantly clothed much the same as Zelda. Then at herself.

"You three look as if you should be in a documentary about the history of the space program," Salem drawled.

Sabrina pointed at Salem. A kitty-cat-size pair of goggles covered two-thirds of his face. "Blast off with us!" Hilda cried, laughing.

"Let's go to the planet of fish, can we please, huh?" Salem begged.

Sabrina scratched her cheek. "I've never heard of the planet of fish."

"It doesn't exist," Salem admitted. "But you can conjure it up for All-You-Can-Cast Day." He swished his tail as he stared pleadingly up at her. "Meow?"

"We'll see," Zelda said, pointing at the broom closet. It opened and the vacuum cleaner flew front and center and parked delicately on the floor. "Aunt Louisa?" she called.

"Oh, is she coming?" Sabrina asked excitedly. Her many-times-great Aunt Louisa lived in a portrait hanging on the wall of their dining room. It would do her good to stretch her legs and gain a new perspective on things.

"I don't know. She talked about it, but she was pretty sketchy," Zelda said. "She told me to pencil her in."

"Go ahead, girls," Aunt Louisa called back. "Leo da Vinci just came by, and we're going to have a nice picnic in a painting by Georges Seurat."

"Are you sure?" Sabrina said. "You don't get out much."

"I'm fine, dear. Go ahead and tour the universe without me."

"All right." Sabrina smiled at her aunts. "Let's go!"

She and Hilda hopped back onto Vacuum Force One. Salem curled up on the base of the other vacuum cleaner while Zelda jumped on behind him and cried, "Contact!"

The vacuum cleaners zoomed out the door and arced into the sky.

"Next stop, the planet of fish!" Salem shouted.

But they didn't go to the planet of fish. They went to the planet of skiing, which was Mars, and slalomed down the slopes on their vacuum cleaners. Then out to Venus for facials, and on to the Milky Way for smoothies.

In the outer rings of Jupiter they met a bushel of German apple witches who were also celebrating the holiday with a grand tour of the universe. The German witches offered the Spellmans tips on how to control their garden gnomes. It seemed this was a pretty severe problem in the region of Germany called the Black Forest, one of the apple witches explained to them.

Apple witches were all dried up and crinkly, but they smelled terrific.

"Danke schön," Zelda said politely. She was fluent in approximately six hundred languages, give or take a dialect or two. Sabrina was having trouble with her two foreign languages—Spanish and Witchese—she was learning the old-fashioned way. "And what can we offer you in return?"

"I have a great invisible closet recipe," Hilda offered.

"Nein, nein. Ve need spell recipes to conjure dead American TV stars," the oldest and plump-

est of the apple witches told her. "You know how
ve thrive on American culture."

"Oh, of course," Hilda said, looking surprised,
but pointing a recipe card into existence. It was
headed FROM THE SPELLMAN KITCHEN, and there
was a cute little drawing of a kitchen witch in the
upper left-hand corner. As the recipe appeared,
one line at time, the witch on the card waved and
winked at Sabrina.

"Aunt Louisa!" she cried.

"Leo had to go home early to invent flight,"
the drawing said. "I thought I'd catch up with
you girls."

Hilda finished the card, reread it, frowned,
and handed it to Zelda. "Do we do this one by
the full moon?" she asked.

"The new moon." Zelda pointed at the card
for the correction.

"How many degrees?"

"Three hundred and fifty. But that's Fahren-
heit, of course."

Hilda presented the card to the head apple
witch with a flourish.

"*Ja*, that's a good one," the witch said appre-
ciatively. She turned to her group. *"I Love Lucy!"*

One of the other witches clapped her hands
and said, *"Ach, gut.* 'Lucy, I'm home!'" The
other witches bobbed their heads and laughed.

"Next time you're in Munich, stop by for
some strudel *mit* us und die Ricardos."

"We'll be sure to. That would be wonderful," Zelda said. She, Sabrina, and Hilda hopped on their vacuum cleaners. *"Auf Wiedersehen! Happy Castanalia!"*

"Babaloo!" the apple witches chorused.

The Spellmans toured most of the known universe, gathering a few more spell recipes from other witches celebrating the holiday. Soon their own recipe box was bulging.

"But not a single recipe for sushi," Salem lamented.

"These are spell recipes, Salem," Hilda said, exasperated. "You know the old saying: 'Teach a witch to fish, and she can feed herself for eternity. Teach a witch to make sushi, and she has to make something else for dinner the next night.'"

"Clunky, and untrue," Salem said, licking his paws. "I'm sure you can make everlasting sushi just like you can make everlasting spaghetti."

"Everlasting spaghetti?" Sabrina echoed, dodging an asteroid. "How come we've never had that?"

"Because you end up with everlasting leftovers," Hilda and Zelda said in one voice, cackling.

"Last one home's a rotten apple!" Sabrina shrieked, leaping off the vacuum cleaner and onto a shooting star. It screeched through the atmosphere, but her aunts trailed close behind.

"Cheater, cheater, cheater!" Hilda shouted merrily at her.

Sabrina dropped off the shooting star and zapped herself into the kitchen. Just as her aunts flew through the open door, she pelted them with Moon Pies. They shouted in mock dismay as the frothy concoctions covered their clothes and faces.

"We'll get you for that!" Hilda said as she and Zelda flung Plutonian puff pastries at Sabrina. Within seconds Sabrina was a sticky statue of glowing green goo and whipped cream.

"I'll get you back double!"

Back and forth the food flew, until the three witches were conducting not a food fight but an all-out food war.

Then Sabrina realized she was running out of ammunition and her finger was tired. Beneath a barrage of Belgian waffles and strawberry topping, Sabrina crabwalked backward and pointed open the freezer section of the refrigerator. Strawberry goop ran down her forehead as she took a quick look inside.

"Hey, girlie, lemme out of here," said a voice. Sabrina stuck her head inside the freezer.

"Who are you?" Sabrina asked.

"Name's Chicky. Deep-Freeze Chicky and the Leftovers."

To her astonishment, a frozen chicken stood up and bowed. Around him, various bundles in aluminum foil and freezer bags began to hum the opening bars of the musical *Grease*.

"Aunt Zelda, Aunt Hilda, our food is talking,"

Sabrina said over the wail of pumpkin-pie bombs and ice-cream-cone missiles.

"Not talkin', singin'! Dancin'!" Chicky cried, dropping down on one knee . . . er, drumstick. "Listen to this. Oh, Hammy, how I love ya, how I love ya, my dear old Hammy. With mashed potatoes, rutabagas, and spuds! My life with you is never a dud!"

"Wow!" Sabrina stepped back and opened the freezer wide. The food came cascading out, landing on the floor. Boxes of frozen peas and mixed vegetables formed a chorus line while Deep-Freeze Chicky pivoted in the middle, singing at the top of his voice: "I got ground beef right here, directly from the steer, and if you put it on defrost, it'll probably cheer!"

"Canned food, canned food," Hilda and Zelda sang, coming up behind Sabrina. "This chick knows about canned food!" They waltzed around the kitchen, completely covered from head to toe in a rainbow of food.

"Sabrina, sing!" Hilda said. "This is the food musical revue version of *Guys and Dolls*. It's called *Beans and Franks*."

Sabrina shouted, "Whoo-hoo!" and joined in the fun. She didn't know the lyrics to the song, or the melody, either, for that matter, but she hummed along, joining in the waltz as they slid through whipped cream, berries, and chocolate.

"Lasagna!" Hilda trilled to the tune of "Maria" from *West Side Story*. "I just ate a piece of lasagna! And suddenly I see, how savory the sauce can be!"

Salem, coated with chocolate syrup and looking for all the world like a big piece of Easter candy, sat on the counter and licked his paws.

"Come on, Salem!" Sabrina urged. "Have some fun."

"I have too much dignity," he said in a snooty voice. Then he burped. "Besides, I had to clean up the mess the fish sticks were making."

"Ida-hoedown!" Zelda shouted, grabbing Sabrina's hands and twirling her in a circle. "Mashed and fried, sake's alive!" Suddenly they were both wearing square-dance skirts. Hilda stood on a bale of hay, playing a fiddle. She played faster and faster, and Zelda whirled Sabrina harder and harder, until they both tumbled into the mountains of food and fell back, laughing. Zelda moved her hands and feet. "We're making food angels!"

"We're going to have to point like crazy to clean this up!" Sabrina said, sitting up. "Oh, that's right, we don't have to! It'll disappear at midnight."

"Let's hope so," Hilda said, zapping her fiddle back into nonexistence. "But you know, it might be the one thing—"

She was cut off by the startling appearance of Sabrina's third aunt, Aunt Vesta.

"Sabrina, darling!" she cried, sliding across the muck on the floor. She slammed into Sabrina, then held on to the counter tightly. As she looked around, she exclaimed, "What a delightful mess!"

"Aunt Vesta!" Sabrina said, wiping whipped cream from her forehead as she struggled to her feet. "How nice of you to drop by."

Much flashier than her two sisters, Vesta lived in the Pleasuredome in the Other Realm, and she really knew how to party. She was wearing a ruby-red strapless evening gown and oodles of rubies and diamonds. (Definitely *not* cubic zirconia. Vesta would never be caught dead in artificial gems.)

"It's all over the cosmos that you're having a smashing time," Vesta said to Sabrina. "I just had to leave the Castanalia Ball at Marigold's to see. And it's true! Finally you're experiencing your true heritage!"

Hilda and Zelda pursed their lips in prim aunt-style frowns. "Sabrina understands that it's just for this one day," Zelda said.

Hilda nodded. "Yes." Then she added, "Marigold had a party? How come we weren't invited?"

"But it doesn't have to be for only one day," Vesta insisted, giving her beautiful hair a toss. "In the Pleasuredome we live like this all the time."

"Sabrina's been there and done that," Zelda reminded Vesta. In fact, Sabrina had spent a weekend with Vesta in the Pleasuredome. "And then she decided to live in this realm with her mortal friends and with us."

"But that was before today," Vesta said pointedly. "I imagine that right about now you're feeling like poor little Cinderella, dear Sabrina." She looped some of Sabrina's long blond hair around her ear. "At midnight, your spells will shatter and you'll turn into a pumpkin!"

"Are you casting a spell or using a really stupid metaphor?" Hilda broke in, a little concerned.

"I think it was a simile," Zelda said. "Now, Vesta, don't confuse Sabrina. She knows what she wants."

"Are you sure, honey?" Aunt Vesta touched Sabrina's shoulder. Her smile was kind. Vesta might be kind of wild, but she did have a good heart. Sabrina knew she really did love her and wanted her to be happy.

"Um, yeah," Sabrina said. "Like they say, 'Half the fun is knowing when to stop.'"

Vesta rolled her eyes. "Oh, *please*. Who on earth says that? It's patently untrue."

"I said it," Zelda said. "And it *is* true. Too much of a good thing—"

"There is no such thing as too much of a good thing," Vesta insisted. She checked her diamond watch. "My, how time flies when you're having fun. Which, in my case is all the time!" She chucked Sabrina under the chin. "I'm going back to my party, Sabrina. But any time you get tired of it all, you just let Aunt Vesta know."

"I will," Sabrina promised.

Poof! Vesta was gone.

"Why didn't we get invited?" Hilda pouted. "We're fun."

"Oh, yeah. Loads," Salem drawled. "Here it is, fifteen minutes to midnight, and all I have to show for Castanalia is one lousy box of frozen fish sticks."

"And a lot of good memories, Salem," Zelda admonished him.

"You can't live on memories, Zelda," Salem retorted. "Believe me, I've tried."

"But that's when you were dieting," Hilda reminded him. She yawned. "Well, I think I'll turn in. Sabrina, it was a wonderful Castanalia. Thank you, dear." She gave Sabrina a hug.

Zelda kissed her on the cheek. "Yes, Sabrina. It's so nice to have you here. We get to reexperience all the witchy first times vicariously through you."

"Good night, Aunt Hilda, Aunt Zelda," Sabrina said as the two sisters left the kitchen.

She turned to Salem. "I have time for one more spell, Salem. And I'll use it for you." She pointed in the direction of the back door.

"Fur that walks
Is fur that talks!"

"Hey, handsome," said a sexy feline voice somewhere outside in the yard.

"Who? What?" Salem asked excitedly.

Sabrina opened the door. "Go get 'em, tiger," she said, giggling.

"And I am outta here!" Salem cried.

Sabrina chuckled. Then she glanced up at the kitchen clock. It was five minutes to midnight. All-You-Can-Cast Day was nearly over. All in all, it had been an amazing day. Smiling, she said softly, "Have fun, Salem," blew on her finger, and pretended to slip it into a holster. It was time to mosey on up to bed. Even witches need their zzzzz's.

☆

Chapter 5

☆

One minute to go until All-You-Can-Cast Day was over.

Making her way through the caloric war zone that had once been the kitchen, Sabrina wiped her feet off at the entrance to the foyer and headed for the stairs. Halfway up, her bomber jacket transformed into her nightgown and her goggles disappeared.

"Oh, that's right," she said, laughing and touching her bare head. She had never actually gotten dressed, so now that all the spells were undone, she was wearing what she'd started the day in.

It was chilly in the house. She grabbed her robe on the way to the bathroom, where she washed her face and brushed her teeth. Then she headed back to her bedroom.

Just then there was a flash, followed by a puff of smoke. She blinked as the Quizmaster, wearing a party hat and holding a noisemaker, sat in her bay window and gave her a wave.

"Hi," she said halfheartedly.

"Did you have fun?" he asked.

"Wait a second," she protested. "Am I being graded on all this?"

He sighed heavily. "You know, before I got this job, I worked for a large corporation in the Other Realm. We went through all that downsizing stuff, and guess who had to hand out the pink slips. You know, lay people off. Fire them."

"I know about pink slips," Sabrina said.

"Okay. I don't mean to talk down to you," he said. "My point is, every time someone who worked for that corporation saw me coming, they'd break down and cry. They thought I was going to fire them. They either feared or hated me." He rolled his eyes. "I knew exactly how Drell must feel."

"And?" Sabrina pressed.

"Well, it's like that with us," he said patiently. "Every time you see me, you think there's going to be a quiz."

"Well, that's because there usually has been."

"Oh." He took that in. "Well, really and truly, I just popped by to see if you had a good time."

"Quizmaster, I'm touched," she admitted. "And the answer is yes. I did. It's a wonderful holiday."

"I agree." He crossed his legs. "Tell me about everything you did. I went to this fabulous party Marigold gave and—"

"How come we didn't get invited?" Sabrina pouted.

He shrugged. "I'm sure you did. Marigold said every witch and warlock got an invitation."

"She snubbed us!" Sabrina cried.

"No." He grinned. "Marigold has a new warlock boyfriend, very powerful, very handsome. She would never miss a chance to lord it over your two single aunts." He thought for a moment. "She said she had Amanda send all the invitations, and—"

"Mystery solved," Sabrina interrupted, slightly downcast. Cousin Amanda couldn't stand Sabrina. Then she brightened. "Well, we couldn't have had any more fun than we did. We went all over the universe, and I was Harvest Queen!"

"Fantastic." He looked pleased. "Tell me," he said. "What was your one thing?"

She blinked at him. "My what?"

He laughed easily. When she didn't laugh back, he cocked his head. "Sabrina, you do know about the one thing, don't you?"

She licked her lips. Had she known, but forgotten? She couldn't remember. It had been a big day.

He tsk-tsked. "Sabrina, Sabrina, Sabrina," he intoned.

"Quizmaster, Quizmaster, Quizmaster," she replied anxiously.

"Whew. What a mouthful. I gotta get a nickname." He leaned forward, suddenly very serious. "Didn't your aunts tell you about the one thing?"

Sabrina tried to think. They'd waited for her to wake up. Then they'd come in to tell her about Castanalia. Next the Witches' Book of the Month Club selections had arrived. Then she'd gone to school and conjured up happy days for everybody, and then they'd gone on their whirlwind tour and had their food fight.

"I'm positive no one told me about the one thing," Sabrina said firmly. She smiled weakly. "So here's your big chance."

The Quizmaster clapped his forehead. "Oy, vey," he said. He pointed his finger. Immediately Hilda and Zelda appeared. Hilda's face was lathered with a bright lavender facial mask and Zelda had been in the process of plucking her eyebrows.

"Hey!" they both protested.

"Quizmaster, it's awfully late, and Sabrina's had a long day," Zelda said. "Whatever you want to ask her, can't it wait?"

"It's not Sabrina I want to question." He narrowed his eyes. "Okay, ladies. Be honest. Did you forget to tell Sabrina about the one thing?"

"No, of course not," Zelda answered at once.

Hilda put her hand on her sister's arm. "Zelda, oops. We did."

Zelda was still speaking. "Because we take our responsibilities toward Sabrina very seriously, and we would never forget . . ." Zelda looked worriedly at Hilda and trailed off. "We did?"

The Quizmaster nodded. "You did."

"Well, it's probably not that big a deal," Hilda said, making a face. "Um, we'll just figure out what didn't get undone tonight and undo it first thing in the morning." She crossed to the window and pulled back the curtains. "Oh, good. The world's still there. That wasn't it."

The Quizmaster folded his arms across his chest. "You know the rules."

"But it's our fault for not telling her about it," Zelda pointed out.

"No one has still not told me about it!" Sabrina exclaimed, and paused. "Was that a real sentence? What I mean is . . ."

"That you haven't the foggiest notion of what we're talking about," the Quizmaster filled in. "Well, it's this, Sabrina. All the spells you cast during Castanalia automatically undo, just like your aunts told you." He frowned at the two sisters. "But what they forgot to tell you is that one spell *doesn't* undo."

She waited. When he said nothing, she moved her shoulders and asked, "Okay. Which one?"

Hilda and Zelda looked at each other. "That's just it, dear," Zelda said. "We don't know."

"We don't know?" Sabrina echoed.

Hilda spread her hands as she began to talk quickly. "See, what most witches do is cast a search-and-destroy spell before Castanalia begins. Then the spell that didn't undo is taken care of by that spell, at one second after midnight. I did it. Didn't you, Zel?"

"Of course," Zelda replied.

"But I didn't," Sabrina said slowly. "Because I didn't know I was supposed to."

The two sisters looked at each other. "We're very sorry, dear," Zelda said, looking contrite. "We overlooked it, somehow. It was very remiss of us."

"But we'll help you find it," Hilda said.

Zelda looked appealingly at the Quizmaster. "You've really got to let us step in. Who knows what spell is still in effect? It could have serious repercussions in this realm."

"I agree," Hilda added.

Zelda went on. "This is no time for some little quiz. We need to take action right away."

" 'Some little quiz'?" the Quizmaster repeated in a hurt tone. "Some little quiz? Do I need to remind you that giving my students these little quizzes is the way—the *only* way—I make a living?"

"He used to fire people," Sabrina offered.

"I hope he can't fire us," Hilda murmured.

Zelda dug her in the side with her elbow. "We can't be fired. We're Sabrina's blood relations."

Hilda didn't look convinced. She chewed on her fingernail and said, "At the very least we'll probably be hauled up before the Witches' Council."

"Probably," the Quizmaster said, nodding. "But for now, let's get to work and figure out which spell didn't undo. We can worry about suspending your witches' licenses later."

"What!" Sabrina cried. "That's not fair!"

"Maybe if we correct the problem quickly, we can avoid any legal problems?" Zelda suggested.

"You can't do anything," the Quizmaster told her.

"That's right," Hilda said. "It must be undone by the witch who cast it, or it won't reverse."

The Quizmaster nodded. "Don't forget the rest: If she doesn't reverse the spell by the next full moon, it will become permanent. No matter what it is, it will never be reversed."

"And no one can ever undo it?" Sabrina echoed, shocked. "Not even the Witches' Council, by turning back time or something?"

"Not even," the Quizmaster said. "Am I right, ladies?"

Hilda and Zelda looked very worried. "I forgot about that part," Hilda admitted.

"I did, too," Zelda said.

Sabrina blurted, "How long have I got?"

Her aunts both groaned. The Quizmaster shook his head at them both. "Haven't you explained to her how important it is for witches to know the precise dates of all full, new, and blue moons?"

"There's an awful lot to learn," Hilda said. "Rome wasn't built in a day, you know."

"It would have been, if I'd been around," the Quizmaster retorted smugly. "Sabrina, for your information, the next full moon is this Friday. You have five days, counting the real today, which is tomorrow." He snapped his fingers. "My error, sorry. It's after midnight, so today is today."

"I'm getting dizzy," Sabrina said. "And to think when I got up, all I knew about Friday was that Harvey wanted to start in the football game."

"The point is, you'd better get cracking," the Quizmaster told her.

Zelda pointed. Instantly everyone was dressed in sweaters and slacks. An enormous pencil materialized in front of Sabrina, along with a pad of paper.

"Write down all the spells you can remember casting," Zelda told her.

Yawning, Sabrina crossed to her nice, fluffy bed and plopped onto it. She was bone-tired, but it sounded as if there was going to be no rest for the weary tonight. She said to the pencil, "First, Hilda conjured my favorite outfit. Then I went to school on a supertemporal skateboard. I let

Harvey ride it, and then I made him float down to earth so he wouldn't end up as flat as a pancake."

"A wise precaution," the Quizmaster said approvingly.

Sabrina yawned again. "We're going to be here all night. I pointed a million times!"

Hilda said, "Wait. There were lots of spells we already know ran their course. For example, though it pains me to announce it, I have been impeached from my office as leader of the free world."

Sabrina grinned at the memory of Hilda as President. She said, "Now you have something in common with Salem."

Hilda drawled, "Except that he was leader of the enslaved world."

"I was Harvest Queen," Sabrina said wistfully.

"And a very pretty one, too, honey." Hilda patted her. "It could be that you'll be the queen again on Friday. That wouldn't be so bad, would it?"

"Well, you might get unimpeached," Sabrina said. "Maybe you'll be President for the rest of time."

"Oh, dear," Hilda muttered. "I, uh, did a few things that might not be seen in, ah, the most positive of lights. Thinking I wouldn't be back after Castanalia, you see." She got a worried, faraway look on her face. After a few seconds she took a little breath and said, "Ooh. I did a lot of things."

The Quizmaster cocked his head. "Any nuclear missiles flying off to places they shouldn't be? Anything like that?"

Hilda thought for a moment. Then she shook her head. "Illegal fundraising activity, mostly. That kind of thing. I approved a new budget to buy the attorney general some new clothes."

"Well, that's money well spent, I'd say," the Quizmaster replied.

Zelda wagged a finger at him. "Some women are too busy doing important work to worry about the superficial dictates of taste and style. I believe Ms. Reno is one of them."

Hilda cocked her head and shrugged her shoulders. "I don't know about that, big sis. I was a pretty gnarly-looking president, and I'm sure I was busier than she."

"Oh, great. You were busy? Busy with that busy little pointer finger of yours?" The Quizmaster rolled his eyes.

Hilda's silence was answer enough.

"But here's a thought," Zelda said, tapping her chin as she paced the room. "Sabrina cast a spell to make Hilda President. But Hilda cast all her own presidential spells. So doesn't that make them hers?"

"Yes," said the Quizmaster.

"Well, I sent out a search-and-destroy, so I'm covered," Hilda said with relief.

They spent the next hour going through Sabrina's day, pinpointing what spells she had cast and if it was already obvious that the spell had been undone. A quick trip to the kitchen took the many spells cast during the food fight off the list. The floor, walls, ceiling, and countertops were spick-and-span.

"The fish sticks are still gone, but Salem really did eat them," Zelda said as they inspected the frozen food. "Nothing magical about that."

"Too bad," Hilda said. "They did a great rendition of 'Sea You in St. Louis.'"

They asked Aunt Louisa if she knew what the rogue spell might be, but she only yawned and said, "Sorry, girls. I don't know anything, and I really need a siesta. I partied hearty all night." Then she shut her mouth and did the Aunt Louisa equivalent of sleeping, which was simply to stare straight ahead like a regular portrait.

"Well, if it's anything you did off the planet, I don't think we should worry too much," Zelda said. "None of us did anything that would have cosmic repercussions that I can think of. I have a feeling it's got to be something here in Westbridge."

"Then I'll go to school in the morning and see what's different," Sabrina suggested. "Then I'll zap it. It shouldn't be too hard."

"Agreed." Zelda clapped her hands. "Let's all try to get some rest. You, especially, Sabrina. You need to be fresh in the morning."

"All right." Sabrina looked at her Quizmaster. "Is this going to go on my permanent record?"

"It'll go on someone's," he said, sliding his glance over at her aunts.

"It's not her fault. We forgot to tell her," Zelda insisted.

The Quizmaster shook his head. "Ignorance of the law is no excuse. Good night, ladies." He snapped his fingers and disappeared.

"Wow, what a tough guy," Hilda said unhappily. She sighed. "I guess we'd all better get some shut-eye. Sabrina, don't worry. We'll figure this out."

Sabrina managed a weak smile. "I know. Good night, Aunt Hilda. Good night, Aunt Zelda." She looked around. "Where's Salem?"

"Outside, I suppose," Hilda said.

Sabrina's aunts left her room. Sabrina crawled into bed and stared at the ceiling. Her mind raced as she replayed her day over and over again. Would Valerie the rock star greet her at her locker? Would Libby still be a nerd? She'd have to wait and see. But she was just too nervous to sleep.

Or so she thought. Before she realized what was happening, Sabrina rose into a deep, deep sleep.

☆

Chapter 6

☆

Sabrina bolted upright and tumbled to the mattress.

"I'm up, I'm up," she told the clock, but it didn't stop buzzing. "Hey," she said, and manually turned it off. Cool. The fail-safe was gone.

"No time for a shower," she muttered as she climbed into a pair of pants and a purple sweater, realizing that she was so nervous she hadn't bothered to point herself into her clothes. Then she grabbed a brush to take care of her hair while she rushed around the room, hunting down her books. In all the excitement, she still hadn't studied for her math test. Wouldn't it be wonderful if that A was the one thing that lasted from Castanalia?

"Sabrina, you're making me queasy," Salem

groused from his spot on the bay window. "Stop moving so fast."

"Don't feel so good?" Sabrina asked.

"Oh, that bimbo Maltese you set me up with heard about Marigold's party. So we crashed the last five minutes and made up for lost time." He groaned. "Have you ever had a catnip hang-over?"

"The one and only time I've been a cat, you were there and I just said no," Sabrina told him as she hurried around the room.

She flew downstairs and headed out the door, calling, "Morning! Gotta go!"

"Wait, wait!" Zelda said. "Sabrina, come sit down."

"Can't!"

"Sabrina, we really need to talk to you," Zelda insisted. "It's very important."

"But I have to get to school," Sabrina protested as she walked into the kitchen. Her aunts each had plates of pancakes, but no one, including the flapjacks, was smiling.

Zelda pointed to the toaster. "Read."

"Uh-oh." Sabrina swallowed. They often received messages from the Other Realm via the toaster. She was sure by the demeanor of both her aunts and their pancakes that some bad news had popped up.

Gathering her courage, she got up and crossed to the toaster. She took out an official-looking piece of paper and began to read:

WARNING WARNING WARNING
OFFICIAL WITCHES' COUNCIL MEMO
EYES ONLY

Sabrina looked up. "What does 'Eyes Only' mean?"

Hilda said, "It means not to share the memo with mortals."

"Okay. Top secret. Got it." Sabrina read on.

To: All witches, warlocks, sorcerers, wizards, fairies, garden gnomes, and other magic users

Sabrina glanced up again. "There's such a thing as fairies? Cool!"

"Don't get distracted, dear," Zelda said. "Keep reading."

Re: Magic Blackout
The Witches' Council has received intelligence that Dr. Francisco Imperium, a mortal scientist connected with the Pentagon, will be conducting experiments to determine the existence of magic beginning today at 6:00 A.M., Witches' Standard Time. He is sending researchers to your area.

All magic users are hereby ordered to cease any use of magic for any reason, until Dr. Imperium leaves the area. You will be contacted when this ban is lifted.

Any questions or comments must be sent to the council before 6:00 A.M. After that time, there will be no contact between the Mortal Realm and the Other Realm until further notice.

Sabrina set the memo on the counter. "Oh, my gosh!" she said. "What about my one thing?" She swallowed. "I guess we'd better discuss this with the council."

"We can't." Hilda pointed to their kitchen clock. "It's seven o'clock."

"Oh, no," Sabrina said. "Why didn't you guys wake me up early?" They must have deactivated the fail-safe on her alarm because it had been put there by magic.

"We didn't get the memo until almost six-thirty," Zelda told her.

"Humph. Typical council bureaucracy," Hilda sniffed.

Sabrina ran a hand through her hair. "What am I going to do?"

"Sit down and have some pancakes," Hilda said. She raised her hand to point, as Zelda said, "Uh-uh-uh. No magic."

"Oooh. This is going to be so weird," Hilda said. "We're actually going to have to cook and walk to places." She looked at Zelda. "I'm not sure I'll be able to last an entire day without using magic."

Sabrina looked at the memo one more time.

At the bottom of the page was a line that either she hadn't noticed or had just appeared:

Unauthorized use of magic will result in the complete removal of the offender's powers and a sentence of no less than one hundred years of existence as an animal of the council's choosing.

"Look at this," she said, showing her aunts.

"Yow," Hilda said.

"Harsh," Sabrina agreed. She walked to the refrigerator and peered inside. There was a carton of milk, some pomegranates for Aunt Hilda, who loved them, and a loaf of bread. She pulled out the milk and bread and studied them. It hadn't been so long since she'd made breakfast for herself that she couldn't rustle a little something up.

"Do we have any cereal?" she asked.

"Just point up some Happy-O's," Hilda said. Witches were not allowed to conjure name brands. She sighed and rolled her eyes. "Never mind. No magic."

"I think there's some peanut butter in the pantry," Zelda suggested, then added quickly as Sabrina started to put the milk and bread back in the refrigerator, "Sabrina, dear, I know you're worried, but you should eat something. You'll need your strength."

"Don't I know it," Sabrina muttered.

To please her aunts, Sabrina ate a peanut butter sandwich and had a glass of milk. Then she washed and dried her breakfast dishes by hand. They usually cast various kinds of cleanup spells to take care of household chores.

Going through the motions of normal mortal life felt strange to Sabrina, and she realized she had started getting used to the idea that she was a witch. She remembered back to the morning of her sixteenth birthday, when her aunts had told her about her powers. Everything had seemed so unreal. Casting spells had taken all the concentration she had. Now, not using magic required just as much effort, and acting like a mortal seemed unreal.

"This is going to be such a strange day," she told her aunts. Zelda was carefully sweeping the kitchen floor while Hilda was staring unhappily at their coffeepot.

"How do you use this thing?" Hilda muttered.

"Just zap up some Master Coffee," Zelda said, pointing to the microwave. "I know what you mean, Sabrina. It's going to be difficult to avoid using magic. But we must all be very careful. We don't want to end up like Salem."

"Gee, no, we couldn't have that," Salem drawled as he dragged into the kitchen. "Where's the coffee? Man, do I need a pick-me-up."

"We're working on it," Hilda told him.

"Could you please work faster?" He sighed. "Maybe I'll just go back to sleep instead." He flopped on his side and immediately began to snore.

"Maybe we should come with you to school to help you look for the one thing," Zelda suggested.

"But how would I explain what you're doing there? Mr. Kraft is very strict about adults checking in with the front office when they're on school grounds."

"We could say you've lost your retainer," Hilda suggested brightly. "Not that you need one, dear." At the skeptical look she received from her big sister and her niece she added quickly, "Or not."

"I think I should go alone, just like usual," Sabrina said. "I guess taking the skateboard is out."

"There's an old unicycle in the basement, if you'd like to use that," Zelda offered.

Sabrina almost laughed out loud. Just what she needed to complete her image as a freak—to show up for school riding a unicycle, just like a circus clown. She said, "Thanks anyway, Aunt Zelda. I think I'll catch the bus." She gave them each a peck on the cheek. "Gotta go!"

As she headed out the door, she heard Zelda say, "It's too bad she didn't want to use the unicycle. Maybe we could give it to Monty's wife." Monty, an old and dear friend of the family, had married a circus contortionist. His familiar had been turned into a newt for trying to help Salem take over the world. "And I suppose we could add a shiny new bicycle to Sabrina's pile of Halloween presents."

Sabrina dawdled in the foyer long enough for Hilda to reply, "My dear, older, sometimes-out-of-it sister, Sabrina's at the age where she doesn't want a bicycle. She wants a car."

"Yes!" Sabrina whispered to herself. *A car for Halloween. Great idea!*

The thought cheered her until she put her hand around the doorknob. Then her nerves took over. With any luck she would find something wrong at school, which she could do nothing to set right. Magically, at least. She crossed her fingers that it was just a little something, and that she could easily fix it in a mortal way.

Then she opened the door.

And stared.

A huge black van was parked at the curb. A metal forest of spinning antennae sprouted from its roof, and a small, curved satellite dish wagged back and forth as if it were trying to signal the mother ship.

"Uh-oh . . ." Sabrina murmured.

Two unsmiling men in black suits stood in front of the van. They wore wraparound sunglasses, so she couldn't tell if they were looking at her or at something else on the Spellman property. One was talking into a walkie-talkie, and the other was speaking into his wrist. He pressed something against his ear and nodded.

Sabrina dashed back into the house.

Her aunts were still in the kitchen. Zelda was bending over the coffee machine, saying, "It's got something to do with all these buttons, Hilda. Maybe I should go check one of my physics books."

"Aunts," Sabrina ventured. "There are—"

"The owner's manual might be more help." Hilda started to point, muttered, "Oh, drat it all," and pushed back from the kitchen table. She crossed to the kitchen counter and pulled open a drawer. "It should be in here somewhere. You never throw anything away. Let's see . . . here's the warranty on our vacuum cleaner. Oh, Zel, it's due for a tune-up. And here's that raffle ticket for a free trip to Funky Town that you bought the first time we were pressured by the fashion industry to wear polyester."

"It was for a good cause," Zelda said. She thought a moment. "I can't remember what it was. But it was a good one."

"Probably the eternal search for a cure for spellfluenza," Hilda said snidely. "Oh, and *this* is useful. Buy one can of Man-Doh, get one free, only it expired twenty-five years ago."

Zelda shrugged and kept fiddling with the coffeepot. "So I missed the date by a few years."

"A few years!" Hilda exclaimed.

"Hello!" Sabrina cried, then bit her lip as they both turned to look at her.

"I thought you'd left for school, dear," Zelda said.

Sabrina put her finger across her mouth. She joined them beside the kitchen counter and whispered, as softly as she could, "There are spooky guys outside."

"Oh, phantoms?" Zelda asked in a loud voice. "Good. That's my ride to the imaginary numbers lecture at the university. I was going to fly over there, but since we can't use magic, I . . ." She trailed off, peering at Sabrina. "What's wrong?"

Sabrina made a "hold-it" gesture with both her hands and rummaged in the same drawer Hilda had been looking through. She found a memo pad from a local real estate company— they were always after the Spellmans to sell; Sabrina didn't know if that was because they figured they could make a lot of money on the house, or they wanted the strange family out of the neighborhood so that property values would rise.

She wrote on the pad, "Not spooky guys woo-woo-woo. Government agents. I think we've been invaded by that scientist. Our house may be bugged."

Silently the two sisters looked first at each

other, then at Sabrina. Sabrina jerked her thumb over her shoulder and led the way back to the parlor.

They lined up to one side of the window, and Zelda pulled back the curtain.

The lawn and walkway were swarming with men and women in somber suits with somber faces. Some held strange pieces of equipment that looked like old-fashioned Geiger counters. Others were sweeping the ground with a close cousin of the metal detector. Others were talking into phones, wrists, and what looked to be tape recorders.

"Eek," Hilda said anxiously. "Should we expect peasants with torches anytime soon?"

Zelda made a calming gesture and turned to them. She whispered, "Be honest. Has either of you cast any spells this morning? Even a tiny one?"

Sabrina wanted to be completely truthful, so she thought through all her actions. She could think of no action she had taken that could be classified as a spell. Satisfied, she shook her head. So did Hilda.

"Then I think we're in the clear," Zelda said. "I think they're just snooping." She straightened her shoulders. "And as a taxpayer, I don't think I have to put up with this kind of invasion of my privacy! I'm going to march right out there and tell those people to pack up."

"No, Zelda," Hilda said. "We should act as inconspicuous as possible."

Zelda looked at her. "Hilda, what self-respecting American mortal would allow all this garbage on his or her lawn? The first thing they'd do is tell them to go away."

"You have a point," Hilda said. She looked at Sabrina.

"She has a point," Sabrina agreed.

"Maybe we should all go," Hilda suggested.

They moved away from the wall, marched through the parlor and into the foyer, and sailed out the front door.

"I'll do the talking," Zelda said.

Hilda muttered, "Why break a trend?"

Either ignoring Hilda, or so engrossed in her task that she didn't hear her sarcastic remark, Zelda marched toward the swarm of black suits and waved her hand. "Good morning," she began. "May I please ask what on earth you're doing?"

A very young man in Ray-Bans and a dark blue suit closed up a notebook and walked toward the three witches. He said, "Ma'am, we're very sorry to disturb you, but a homicidal maniac is on the loose."

"In Westbridge?" Zelda feigned utter shock. "But we're such a nice little town. Such a nice, *quiet* little town."

"Such a nice, quiet, *boring* little town," Hilda

added helpfully. "Where nothing strange ever happens. A maniac would bypass us in favor of, oh, say, Salem."

"Or Boston," Sabrina broke in quickly. She didn't think this was the time to mention nearby Salem, the witchy HQ of the eastern seaboard. "Boston is where all the really insane killer-types go. More victims."

"Better-dressed ones, too," Hilda said.

Just then an older man approached them. Sabrina was positive that he had never, ever smiled in his entire life, and he didn't look like today was going to be any different.

"Ms. Zelda Spellman?" he said to Zelda.

Zelda raised her chin. "Yes?" she responded rather imperiously, as if unsmiling men in suits approached her every day.

He turned to Hilda. "Ms. Hilda Spellman?"

"Yes?" She tried to imitate Zelda's cool and collected tone, but her voice came out somewhere between a haughty reply and a mouselike squeak.

He turned next to Sabrina. "Ms. Sabrina Spellman?"

Sabrina said, "What!" way too loudly.

"Please come with me. There's something we need to discuss."

The three Spellmans looked at one another.

"Uh-oh," Hilda murmured.

Zelda cleared her throat meaningfully and dug Hilda in the ribs.

"Sabrina has to get to school," Zelda informed the man.

"Westbridge High," the man said, as if ticking information off a list. Or a rap sheet for one of America's Most Wanted. "Don't worry, ma'am. We'll take care of that."

Like prisoners heading off to the Big House, the trio of witches followed the unsmiling man.

Chapter 7

☆

☆

As Sabrina and her aunts followed the somber man in black, they stared in amazement at all the commotion on their once-peaceful street. Besides the van parked outside their house, there was another one inching up the street, its antennae twirling like a slow-motion top. An unsmiling woman stood under the shade of an oak tree and talked into a pen. A man wearing latex gloves crouched beside the fire hydrant, scraping up bits of grass and depositing them into an envelope marked EVIDENCE.

Hilda said in an under voice, "Maybe this is someone else's *one thing*. You know, a practical joke by a witch for witches."

"We can hope," Sabrina replied. If that were the case, the joke wasn't very funny, and was getting less so as the man gestured for them to turn to the right and enter the van with the twirling antennae, which had pulled up to the curb. Besides, that memo from the Other Realm had looked pretty authentic to her.

"Please enter," their grim escort said as the van door opened. A soldier dressed in a Marine Corps uniform blocked the door. He carried a rifle across his chest, and there was a huge, wicked-looking gun in a holster at his side.

"At ease, soldier," the man said. He flashed him a badge.

"Sir, yes, sir." The soldier relaxed a bit and stood aside.

Zelda glanced at the others and climbed the first three steps into the vehicle. Hilda and Sabrina followed close behind.

"Wow," Sabrina breathed.

"Yeah, double wow," Hilda agreed.

The large van interior was dimly lit and packed with people and electronic equipment. People sat at half a dozen screens of some sort, murmuring and pointing at readouts and strange images which moved and dipped. Machines buzzed and clicked. A printer spewed out a page. A fax machine—or something like it—went off. Everyone was drinking coffee out of Styrofoam cups, edging around each other in the crowded space, murmuring, "Excuse me. Lisa, catch that blip? There's something. What's that, another anomaly?" Machines buzzed, clicked, and whirred. Maybe they *could* detect the presence of magic.

Maybe they already had.

"Are these the new assistants?" someone asked in a harried voice. "Good, good. As usual, we're understaffed. How can they expect good work out of me when they don't give me enough tools?"

Rushing forward from the shadows, a man with blue-black hair that zigzagged with white at the temples, extremely bushy black eyebrows, and a pencil-thin mustache approached them, his head down as he ticked items off a clipboard. "Just take off your coats." He looked up. "You're not wearing coats. Oh, you're . . . *oh.*" His dark blue eyes flashed as he stared at Zelda.

Zelda put her hands on her hips and said angrily, "Dr. Imperium, I presume?"

"Why, yes." His mouth hung open as he gaped at her as if she were the most beautifully ravishing woman in the universe. "And you are?"

"Zelda Spellman." Raising her chin, she said, "And I demand to know why we have been detained."

"Detained?" The man shook his head most earnestly. "Oh, I assure you, no detention is meant." Zelda huffed and crossed her arms. He went on. "As I'm sure Special Agent Covey explained to you, we're looking for a homicidal maniac."

"From Mars?" Hilda blurted. "C'mon, we've

seen far too many episodes of *The X-Files* to fall for a lousy story like that."

"Then I'm sure you can understand our need for discretion," said another man as he walked from the shadows. He was short and squat, and he wore a khaki military uniform jacket covered with medals and ribbons.

"Who are you?" Zelda asked boldly as she glared at the new man, but her voice shook just a little.

"I'm Colonel Van De Ven," he announced, sticking out his chest. In the dull green light from the monitors, his medals gleamed strangely. "And your last name is *Spell*-man." He said it slowly, distinctly pronouncing each syllable. "Unusual name."

"It's from our English heritage. Our ancestors were men who could spell," Hilda supplied.

"All the men in our family are excellent spellers," Sabrina added helpfully. "They win spelling bees left and right."

"Most unusual," Van De Ven observed.

"What's so unusual?" Hilda asked.

He looked at all three of them with a weird little smile. "Well, as you know, males are generally more skilled in theoretical abstraction—subjects such as math and science, while females tend to excel in verbal ability. Such as spelling."

Zelda frowned. "Oh, is that so? I happen to be a physicist."

81

"And I happen to be a lousy speller," Hilda added, equally insulted.

Sabrina nodded. "That's true. She's worse than I am."

Hilda nodded brightly.

"Now, come clean," Zelda insisted. "What are you really doing here?"

"Well, Ms. Spellman," Dr. Imperium said, smiling goofily at her. He inhaled slowly, then exhaled. "What's that perfume you're wearing?"

Zelda cocked her head. "I beg your pardon?"

"It smells wonderful. Oh, Ms. Spellman . . . Zelda, if I may . . ." He blushed. "We're here to investigate the possible existence of something wonderful." He sighed as his gaze swept her face. "Something truly beautiful—"

"Toxic waste," Colonel Van De Ven said, clearing his throat. "And we're enlisting your aid as block captains. We request that you monitor your area and report any suspicious activity to us."

Zelda looked at him. "Such as what? Our neighbors dumping their trash?"

"Anything you think is out of the ordinary," Colonel Van De Ven said. "That is all."

"That is all?" Zelda echoed incredulously.

"Yes, ma'am." The colonel nodded to the sentry, who snapped to attention. "Please escort these civilians out."

"Yes, sir," the soldier said. He looked down at

Sabrina. He was very young and kind of cute, actually, now that she could see his face. "Miss, if you please. Watch your step."

Sabrina swallowed and nodded.

Before they could leave, Dr. Imperium touched Zelda on the arm. "If I may," he said, "I'd like to share my findings with you." He paused. "If I find any."

"That would be very nice," Zelda replied. "Now, goodbye."

The three witches stepped down and out of the van.

Behind them Dr. Imperium said, "Colonel, why did you lie to that beautiful woman and her family? Toxic waste, indeed. As soon as my detection meters pick up magic trace emissions, the entire world will know why we're here!"

"They don't need to know anything right now," the colonel replied. "I'm suspicious of those three. There's something about them. Not counting the fool you're making of yourself over the oldest one."

"Nonsense," the doctor said. "They're harmless New England middle-class women. And she's not old at all," he added dreamily.

Zelda looked askance at Hilda, who looked askance at Sabrina, who blew her bangs off her forehead and said, "Phew. I'd say that was close, except I don't think it was. This is all a bunch of pseudoscientific nonsense. I'm going to go to school and fix my one thing with magic."

"Shh, Sabrina, keep your voice down!" Zelda admonished her. "We're under a ban from the Witches' Council itself. If you violate that ban, you'll pay the price."

Sabrina crossed her arms over her chest. "But there's no need—"

"Maybe there is, maybe there isn't," Zelda persisted. "It doesn't matter, Sabrina. Point that finger, and your powers are history."

"All right, all right." She was irritated. "They don't have to push us around like that." She reddened. "Not the council, I mean. These mortal guys."

"Yeah," Hilda said. "They don't." She nudged Zelda. "Maybe if you ask Dr. Imperium extra nicely, he'll just leave. He certainly has a crush on you." She sniffed the air. "Are you wearing Simply Irresistible? Because I think that would count as using magic, Zelly." Simply Irresistible was a perfume that made the wearer, well, simply irresistible. A witch could only buy it in the Other Realm.

"No, I'm not. It's just that nice soap Sabrina bought for me last Halloween." Zelda smiled sweetly at Sabrina. "And it was a lovely gift, dear."

"Well, as soon as the ban is lifted, we'll get out our number 10 cauldron and make a big pot of revenge," Hilda said. "I refused to be pushed around by the military-industrial complex in the sixties, and I refuse to now."

"All right," Zelda said. "But for now, we must lie low."

"Block captains." Hilda snorted. "If they only knew that what they're looking for is right under their noses!"

"Shh." Zelda put a warning finger to her lips. "Someone might overhear us."

"Yes. Because they hid microphones in our clothing," Hilda said angrily as she stomped along. "Honestly, the way that man was staring at you was enough to make me drink some Man Brew and thrash him."

"It does make things a little more complicated for us," Zelda agreed.

"A little?" Hilda repeated.

"Well, it's not my fault." Zelda started to point at Hilda, then remembered herself and folded her hands together. "C'mon. We have chores to do. And they're going to take us all day, I'm afraid."

"Just remember, no windows," Hilda shot back. "I didn't do them when they were invented, and I don't do them now."

Still squabbling, Sabrina's aunts trooped back into their house.

Sabrina headed off for school. The unsmiling government agents were everywhere, skulking behind trees and hiding around corners. She began to notice a large number of strangers in regular street clothes who were trying to blend in—men on park benches, women pushing baby strollers, a couple of joggers murmuring into their wristbands. It was like being in a spy movie.

A very bad spy movie.

At school another black van was parked with the school buses, and a man in a gym uniform stood beside it. The man was talking to Harvey, who was nodding and making gestures. He held his hand out, as if to indicate how tall someone was. Sabrina's stomach clenched.

As if to indicate how tall she was.

Harvey was such a good-natured guy that he wouldn't hesitate to spill his guts to someone official. It wouldn't occur to him that someone pretending to be a good guy could do an awful lot of harm to someone Harvey cared about.

"But they can't do anything," Sabrina muttered. "The whole thing is stupid."

Harvey saw her, waved, and loped toward her. "Hiya, Sabrina."

"Hey, Harvey. Who was that guy?" she asked.

"A scout," he said excitedly. "He's here to watch football practice." He took a breath. "I'm pretty nervous."

A scout, huh? She looked in the man's direction. Then she realized she'd seen him yesterday at the Castanalia football game. He really *was* a scout. She exhaled and said, "Me, too." Then she shook herself. "Harvey, there's no need for you to be nervous. You're a great player."

He shrugged. "I'm an okay player."

Suddenly a man came out of the van and talked to the scout. Sabrina said absently, "Whatever. I mean, no, you're great!"

"But you like me," Harvey said. "You'd think I was great even if I wasn't."

She kept her eye on the two men as she moved toward the school. Harvey went with her, still chatting about football.

"Let's roll, Harvey," she urged. "I don't want to be late for school." She needed to stay one step ahead of Dr. Imperium and Colonel Van De Ven, find out what her one thing was, and take care of it as discreetly as possible. But how was she going to pull that off in a school full of spies?

She headed off to first period, swinging around the corner just in time to collide with Libby.

Libby, who was not dressed with her usual flair. Who was, in fact, wearing a baggy, ugly dress and whose hair was tied back in a bun. And even more astonishing, muttered, "So sorry, Your Majesty," as everything in Libby's purse careened down the hall and ricocheted off the walls like the balls in a pinball machine.

"Libby, you're my one thing!" Sabrina cried.

"Excuse me?" Libby asked, glaring up at her. "What one thing are you referring to, 'Your Royal Highness'?" Her voice dripped with sarcasm. "I can't believe you would actually even consider running for princess of the Harvest Court. When Valerie told me you had the insane notion of running against me, I nearly fainted with laughter." She grabbed at her lipstick and accidentally rolled it away from herself. "Now look what you made me do, you freak! I'm already late for drama rehearsal."

"I guess I'll cross this cross girl off my list," Sabrina said softly, getting to her feet. It was tempting to point at Libby's lipstick to make it roll all the way down the hall as the other girl scrambled to pick up her errant belongings, but Sabrina kept her fingers to herself.

Valerie appeared at Sabrina's locker, her eyes red from crying. She said, "Oh, hi, Sabrina. Good morning." She sniffled. "Not that it is one."

"Valerie, what's the matter?" Sabrina asked, filled with concern. "What happened? And why did you tell Libby I'm running for Harvest princess?"

Valerie rolled her eyes. "Sometimes I think I'm too stupid to live. You know, sometimes you dare to dream. Or at least, I do. Brian Enders said he wanted to talk to me today. So I got all dressed up, you know? I actually thought he might be thinking of asking me to the dance. Can you believe how dumb I was?"

"That's not dumb at all," Sabrina said, suppressing a grimace. She already knew what was coming.

"Right." Valerie huffed. "The most popular boy in school is going to ask *me* out."

"But he didn't?"

"He asked me to walk Libby's dog. And Libby offered to pay me a dollar an hour!"

"Cheapskate," Sabrina muttered, then more loudly said, "Oh, Valerie, I'm so sorry. You didn't say yes, did you?"

"I did," Valerie wailed. "I did! Libby hinted that she might be nicer to me and tell the other girls on the cheer squad I was nice, and I fell for it hook, line, and sinker! I can't believe myself. I'm so pathetic."

"No. You just want what every other kid in high school wants. To be accepted, and to be liked." Sabrina sighed, contrasting the sad, dejected Valerie standing before her with the cool rock star who had jammed with Elvis, the leader of the free world, and the Harvest Queen. Would it really be so bad to put a little magic in Valerie's life?

Yes.

"Somehow I thought it would impress her if you were running for princess, so I said you were. I know you aren't." She slumped in misery. "I'm sorry. Now she'll be on your case, too."

Sabrina sighed and put her hand on Valerie's shoulder. "Valerie, someday we won't be in high school anymore. Nobody will care that Libby was a bigshot cheerleader and you were . . . *not* a bigshot cheerleader." She smiled brightly. "And being able to say that you were the newspaper editor will go a lot farther on a job application than bragging that you knew how to do the splits." She added softly, "Or that you were a Harvest princess."

Valerie considered Sabrina's words. "I suppose you're right." But she didn't look convinced. "Her dog's some kind of champion. Of *course.* I assume that means he has good doggy manners."

"Or else Abdul is spoiled rotten," Sabrina offered.

Valerie stared at her hopelessly. "How did you know his name? I didn't even know Libby had a dog. I'm so out of the loop!"

"Oh, she mentioned him once in the cafeteria," Sabrina assured her. "I was standing behind her in line."

Valerie looked a little happier, but not much.

The bell rang. Sabrina said, "Gotta go," and took off.

Valerie was not the one thing. Elvis hadn't put in an appearance, so she could cross him off her list, too. Just how many spells had she cast, anyway? It was amazing witches didn't end up with carpal tunnel syndrome.

She looked up just in time to see Mr. Kraft walking down the hall with what had to be another one of the government agents, a somber man in a black suit talking into what had to be a phone, but looked very much like a coffee thermos. He was carrying some kind of meter, and it was ticking like a bomb.

Mr. Kraft looked glassy-eyed, either excited or frightened about having the government guys on campus. The vice-principal glanced at Sabrina, then did a double-take and looked at her again. *Uh-oh. Was the one thing something I did to myself?*

Then the agent spoke to Mr. Kraft. Mr. Kraft answered, and they both continued down the hall.

Sabrina hurried into the nearest girls' bathroom and checked herself out in the mirror. Nothing unusual. Maybe she had accidentally cast a spell that only mortals could see.

"Now you're getting paranoid," she murmured to her reflection.

A serious-faced woman in a black suit and sunglasses came out of one of the stalls. She, too, was holding some kind of meter in her hand. "No, miss, we're just being thorough," the woman said, and ran the meter up and down the outside of the row of stalls. *Tick-tick-tick.* Then she got down on her hands and knees and waved the meter over the floor.

"What are you doing?" Sabrina asked.

"Checking for magicon residue."

Sabrina squinted at the meter. "Magicon?"

"It's a unit of measurement for the energy expended during the casting of a spell. This is a magicometer." She gestured to her instrument.

"Find anything?" Sabrina asked in what she hoped was a polite but interested tone, and what came out instead as a nervous squeak.

"Sorry, miss. That information's classified," the woman informed her as she continued to scan the floor.

Sabrina stared at her, speechless and a little frightened.

92

☆

Chapter 8

☆

Math class.

After the test was over, everyone had to trade papers and grade the answers. Gordie, who had Sabrina's paper, looked across the row from her and gave her a thumbs-up. "You did great!" he told her.

Maybe my one thing really was this A.

If that was the case, it was tempting not to worry too much about undoing it.

School let out. Harvey had practice and Valerie had to go to the dentist, so Sabrina was on her own. She decided she should probably go home and see how her aunts were dealing with the invasion of the magicometers.

As she crossed through a small park, a chipmunk zigzagged from one tree to another, gathering up acorns and then dropping them, as if he couldn't decide which one was the best.

"Hiya, cutie-pie," Sabrina said.

"Who youse callin' cutie-pie?" the chipmunk snapped at her.

She brightened. "Oh, are you someone's familiar?" Most witches had a small animal, called a familiar. Usually it was a cat or dog. Some witches had talking vaccum cleaners. Her aunts had Salem. Then she lowered her voice. "We're supposed to cool it until that mad scientist leaves," she whispered. "Okay?"

"What're youse talkin' about?" the chipmunk demanded, sitting up on his hind legs. "Are youse crazy or what?" He turned his head as he made little chipmunky nibbling noises. "Hey, Lydia! Come on over here."

A second chipmunk scampered over. The first chimpmunk said, "This dame's all in a lather over something."

Sabrina looked around to be sure they were alone, then from one chipmunk to the other. "Have you always been able to talk?" she asked. Maybe it was a secret animals usually kept from humans. Or maybe now that her witchy powers were developing, she was more in tune with them.

"What's she talking about?" the first chipmunk demanded of the other.

The second one said, in a decidedly more

feminine voice, "I dunno, Artie. Talking, what? We're just chipmunks, girlie." She made a nibble-nibble face at the other chipmunk. "Maybe she's from the union. We're members, pay our dues, yadda yadda yadda," Lydia the chipmunk assured her.

"Chipmunks have a union?" Sabrina asked, amazed. The things you learned when you walked home from school!

"We're in the Fraternity of the Fully Furry, Local Number 77," Artie informed her.

"Fully Furry?" She considered that. "Meaning animals with fur?"

"Meaning that precisely." The chipmunk washed his face with his tiny front paws.

"And all furry animals are members?"

"If they ain't scabs," Artie said. "You know, animals that cross picket lines, that sort of thing." He chattered at Lydia, then rubbed his forepaws together. "Speaking of which, I gotta get back to work. The boss don't like us putting in for overtime, and I have a ton of acorns to scatter around aimlessly."

"Oh. Okay," Sabrina said as he darted away.

"Don't mind him, honey," Lydia told her. "He's the nervous kind, know what I mean?" She chittered at Sabrina, zigged, then zagged, and zoomed up a tree.

Sabrina watched them both go. Bemused, she continued walking home.

Across the street a fat Siamese cat looked up from napping in the afternoon sun and drawled, "You're home a little early today, Sabrina dahlink. No vun to hang with at the Slicery?"

"Are you in the Fully Furry union?" Sabrina asked.

The feline licked her shoulder and yawned. "Of course, dahlink. I am, as you can see, absolutely, luxuriously furry."

"How long have you been in it?" Sabrina persisted, growing excited.

"As long as I can remember." The Siamese stretched. "Have you any snacks with you, sweet girlie? Catnip? Caviar? Grey Poupon?"

"No. Sorry."

Wait a minute . . . this had to be it! This had to be her one thing! Now she remembered the very last spell she had cast: *Fur that walks is fur that talks*. Instead of specifying a spell so that Salem could talk to the kitty in the backyard, she had made it possible for all furry animals to speak! The Quizmaster was always after her to be careful with her spell phrasing.

"Uh-oh!" How was she supposed to fix this without using any magic?

"One lump or two, Dr. Imperium?" Hilda asked the scientist. She and Zelda sat side by side in their parlor, acting as if having tea with a man bent on "exposing" the reality of witchcraft was a common everyday occurrence.

Dr. Imperium shook his head. "I don't use processed sugar. It's white death."

Hilda shrugged. "However, it's sweet." Using the sugar tongs their great-great-great-great Uncle Ziven the Seasick had won from Blackbeard the Pirate in a game of dominoes, she dropped not one, not two, but three lumps into her own china cup.

Dr. Imperium playfully wagged his finger and said, "I'll live longer than you will."

Hilda, the centuries-old witch, smiled. "Maybe. Maybe not."

Zelda chimed in, "I'm still not clear how we can help you. You already asked us to be block captains."

"I did some, ah, checking on you," Dr. Imperium said hesitantly. He looked at her adoringly as he clasped his hands together. "You, Zelda Spellman, are a renowned and highly respected physicist."

Zelda preened. "Well, yes, that's true."

"And I, Francisco Imperium, am horribly understaffed. They never give me enough money." He muttered to himself as he accepted his tea from Hilda, "Which is why I never produce any results." Then he said to Zelda in a kinder, gentler voice, "So how would you like to join me in the adventure of a lifetime? A witch hunt?"

Hilda and Zelda both nearly choked on their tea. "Excuse me, Dr. Imperium?" Zelda asked.

"Yes." His eyes gleamed. "I've decided to go

public with you, Ms. Spellman. I sense that I can trust you. You're the kind of woman who can keep secrets. My kind of woman." He cleared his throat and brought himself back to his point. "It's not a homicidal maniac, and it's not toxic waste, it's women in pointy hats with big, ugly warts on their noses."

"Now just a minute," Hilda interjected. "Why is it that everybody assumes—"

"Dr. Imperium, what a kind offer," Zelda cut in, speaking over Hilda. "I'm not sure I have the expertise you require, however. I don't know the first thing about the subject. And my branch of physics is strictly theoretical." She set down her cup and folded her hands in her lap. "I assume you must have proof of the existence of witchcraft to have gotten this far in your field work?"

"Well . . ." He sat up very straight and ran his fingers through the zigzags of silver at his temples. "I had excellent results in the lab."

"Oh?" Zelda asked calmly as both she and Hilda traded little glances. *In the lab?* "Such as?"

Just then the front door burst open. "Aunt Hilda! Aunt Zelda!" Sabrina called, dropping her bag on the chair by the door. "Guess what! I found my one thing! It's—"

She saw Dr. Imperium and screeched to a halt.

"Hello, Sabrina," Zelda said. "You were saying that you found that thing you lost?"

"Yes, my, uh, my unicycle!" she said. "It's in the basement." She laughed. "Right where you said it would be. I checked this morning before I went to school."

"Terrific," Zelda said.

Hilda nodded in agreement and poured herself some more tea. "Peachy-keen. Have some tea, Sabrina. I made it myself. With tea bags and everything."

"This may sound odd, but I rode a unicycle in college," Dr. Imperium said. "I'd love to take a look at yours, Miss Spellman."

Sabrina looked at her aunts, who looked blankly back at her. "Sure," she said cheerily. "I'll just go get it now."

She left the room and climbed the stairs down to the dark, spooky basement. In their centuries of living, her aunts had accumulated a lot of stuff. Old cauldrons and dried herbs hung from the rafters. Wooden chests were stacked nearly to the ceiling, marked 1600s, 1700s, 1800s, and so on. Sabrina was momentarily distracted. *It would be fun to look through all this stuff! Especially the next time I have a history paper . . .*

She wandered past a Hula Hoop, pieces of a broken-down carriage, and an actual glass slipper, cracked and badly reglued. There were some decorations from the Halloween party her aunts had helped her throw, including garlands shaped like pumpkins and a couple of boxes of extra paper plates and cups with cute little bats on them.

But nowhere did she see a unicycle—

"Okay, now, everyone knows their roles?" a voice whispered.

"Could you run through it one more time, Master?" squeaked a tiny voice.

"Okay. Now, listen up. . . ."

Sabrina's lips parted. *Salem!*

"You infantry troops will chew through the telephone wiring at the White House, and you airborne divisions will fly over the Pentagon with this listening device, and—"

"Hello?" Sabrina called, peering around a box with writing on the side that said HILDA'S RECORD COLLECTION, 1950S. DO NOT TOSS.

"Cheese it, it's one of *them*," Salem said quickly.

He was sitting on a box that said YE PARTY FAVORS, 1603. Perhaps a dozen little gray field mice, some chipmunks, and one snow-white rat scattered as Sabrina picked Salem up and looked suspiciously into his eyes.

"Salem, are you by any chance planning another shot at world domination?" she demanded.

Salem blinked innocently at her. "Who, me?"

"And are you by any chance aware that my one thing is that all the furry animals in Westbridge can talk?"

"Meow?" he tried.

"For shame!" Sabrina cried. "I—I should tell the Witches' Council on you."

"No interrealm communications are allowed until that lunatic goes away," Salem said smugly. "And since he's got such a tremendous crush on Zelda, I figure the wedding's just around the corner and he'll be around forever. I'll be world leader before the minister says, 'You may kiss the bride.'"

"Are you out of your mind?" Sabrina cried.

Salem licked his paw. "Hey, I almost pulled it off last time."

"I mean, about Aunt Zelda and that lunatic. I mean, Dr. Imperium."

"'That lunatic' works fine for me—"

"Whatever."

"They're upstairs having *tea*," Salem said smugly.

"Only to be polite. Only because otherwise he might figure out that we're—"

"Find that unicycle?" Dr. Imperium called from the top of the stairs.

"Still looking," Sabrina sang out.

"Here. I'll help you," he said.

Oh, no. He can't come down here and see all this stuff! She started to point at the nearest box, but then Salem hopped down from his perch and trotted up the stairs.

"Oh, no, a cat! Ah-ah-ah-choo!" Dr. Imperium took a white handkerchief from the inside of his lab coat. "I'm allergic to cats."

Salem turned and winked at Sabrina. Then he

continued up the stairs. Sabrina craned her neck to see Salem curling himself around the scientist's legs and meowing sweetly.

"Scat, scat." Dr. Imperium turned and left the basement.

"Saved from the mad scientist by the crazed dictator," Sabrina muttered. She looked around. "Hey, you furry people. Come out here. We need to talk."

"Eee, eek, ee-ee-ee," squeaked a little tiny voice. A mouse, small even for a mouse, skittered over to her and rose on its back legs. "Eee, eek, ee-ee."

Sabrina stooped down and held out her hand. The mouse darted into her palm. It tickled. Sabrina giggled and lifted it toward her face.

The mouse chittered at her. "I said I said I said, where's Fearless Leader?"

"Who? Oh, you mean Salem?" *Fearless Leader, huh*. Sabrina wondered if this little critter knew that Salem often chased mice for the fun of it. "He had to go take care of something. But listen, you guys are going to have to stop talking." She hesitated. "For a few days." She felt kind of guilty saying that; because as soon as Dr. Imperium left, they would stop talking forever . . . with a little help from her.

"Stop stop stop?" The mouse rubbed its front paws together. "No no no way!" He ran up Sabrina's arm and climbed up on her shoulder. "We love love love to talk to humans!"

Uh-oh . . .

"Sabrina, are you all right?" Zelda called.

"Yes, Aunt Zelda." Sabrina said to the mouse, "I'm going to go get Fearless Leader and we'll have a meeting of the entire Furry union, okay? Pass the word."

"Yes, yes, yes!" the mouse squeaked. It darted down her arm and cozied into her palm. It said, "You know, with a little water, this would make a great swimming pool."

"Mmm." She had no answer for that. As she put the mouse back down on the floor, she spied a wheel poking out from behind some more boxes.

"Ah-ha!"

She moved the boxes aside, got the unicycle, and started up the stairs. As she went up, she heard a little voice chirp, "Who's the babe?"

"She works for Fearless Leader," another voice answered.

"Salem, you got some 'splaining to do," she said in her best Ricky Ricardo accent. *But not until Dr. Imperium left their house.*

From the parlor erupted an explosive *"Aah-choo!"*

"Whew, good thing he's not a witch," Sabrina whispered as she met Hilda on the threshold to the basement. "He could start a thunderstorm with those sneezes of his."

"Shh, keep your voice down," Hilda warned, then giggled.

103

"Oh, Dr. Imperium, I'm so sorry about our cat," Zelda said soothingly from the living room. "Let me show you to the door."

"Call me Francisco," he answered, sounding completely love-crazed and very stuffed up. Zelda and the scientist stepped outside, Zelda shutting the door behind them.

"I'd like to turn *him* into a door," Hilda muttered. "'Big, ugly warts—'"

Just then Salem sauntered toward Hilda and Sabrina. Sabrina whirled on him. "So what's the haps, *Fearless Leader?*" she asked pointedly.

Salem coughed into his paw. "Beg pardon?"

"Don't play innocent with me." Sabrina turned to Hilda. "Aunt Hilda, my one thing is that all the furry animals can talk. And Salem's trying to talk them into helping him take over the world again!"

"Salem!" Hilda said, shocked. "Don't you ever learn?"

"You misheard," Salem insisted.

"No, I didn't." Sabrina put her hands on her hips. "One of your little mousie friends ratted on you."

Salem was silent. He hung his head. "What can I say in my defense? This realm would be so much better off if I ran things."

"Knock it off right now or we'll tell the Witches' Council. When we can." Hilda made a face. "And when can we, anyway?"

"Maybe you should sneak into Dr. Imperium's van and make him so sick he has to leave," Sabrina suggested to Salem. "We won't tell the council about your evil plan if you do it."

"That's kind of a temporary solution," Hilda offered. "I think we need to find a way to convince him once and for all that there is no such thing as witchcraft, and most definitely, no witches in Westbridge."

"And I need to find a way to convince all the animals to stay mum until we do," Sabrina said.

"I'm going to go help Zelda get rid of him." Hilda took the unicycle from Sabrina. "Maybe he'll ride this thing into some oncoming traffic." She went off toward the living room.

"Maybe if you *ordered* your troops to be quiet, they would," Sabrina suggested to Salem.

He shook his head. "Are you kidding? Have you guys ever been able to shut *me* up?"

"But, Salem, this is really important," Sabrina insisted. "If Dr. Imperium overhears them—or you!—we're in really big trouble. Especially me," she added weakly. She could just see the headlines in *The Other Realm Gazette:* TEENAGE WITCH CONVICTED OF MAJOR STUPIDITY. POWERS REVOKED.

"I might be able to get my followers to be quiet," Salem mused.

"Yes!" Sabrina cried, clapping her hands.

"But not all the furry animals in town are my followers," he went on. He cocked his head and looked up at Sabrina. "If you could convince them to join with me in crushing the established order—I mean, convince them to listen to the wisdom of Fearless Leader . . ."

"Nice try, but it won't work," Sabrina said. "Is world domination all you think about?"

"That, and lint," he retorted.

Sabrina was getting desperate. "You have to help me, Salem." As much as he was allowed to help, anyway.

Salem's tail flicked about almost eagerly. "What's it worth to you?"

Chapter 9

☆

"This is the pits," Sabrina grumbled as she took out another twenty dollars and handed it to the pet shop clerk. Beside her, a bright red cart was loaded to the top with catnip, rawhide chew bones, hamster kibble, gerbil food, and other assorted treats for furry, greedy little beasts.

"Hey, we have the best prices in town," the clerk retorted.

"Believe me, I know." Pricing pet supplies had become her number-one after-school activity. That and dodging Dr. Imperium's spies, who were everywhere.

Including behind her in line. Six or seven strong-jawed, unsmiling men and women in black suits and sunglasses stood one after another holding bags of dog food, pet shampoo, and flea powder.

"Here's your change," the clerk added, handing Sabrina twelve cents.

Great. That was the last of her savings. In the two days since the arrival of Dr. Imperium, Sabrina had been approached by union representatives of the Fraternity of the Fully Furry, who had informed her that its members were willing to stop speaking in exchange for various treats. And they had just happened to have a list of their tasty demands with them.

"These are bribes!" Sabrina had protested.

"You balk, we talk," the furry rep had retorted.

Now Sabrina took her cache of animal goodies to the appointed rendezvous spots all over town. As she bent with the weight of the enormous plastic sack, she whistled to herself as if carrying something the approximate size and weight of a dead body was something she did every day and should not alarm anyone in the least—

"Excuse me!" A head peeked from around a mailbox. It was a man in a dark suit wearing sunglasses. He was holding a magicometer and pointing it straight at her.

"May I ask you what's in the bag, miss?" he said.

This is becoming routine! "I'm collecting food and toys for the less fortunate among us," she said calmly as she opened the sack. "Less fortunate animals."

"I see." The man appeared satisfied. From his

breast pocket he pulled out a notebook, made a few scribbles, and replaced the notepad. "Please proceed."

She smiled at him and went on her way.

In a clearing in the woods she let the sack fall to the ground and wiped her forehead. *This thing weighs a ton!* But she felt like Santa Claus as some animals tentatively poked their heads out of tree stumps or scrabbled along the ground for the goodies. Talkative or not, they were really cute.

"Hey, girlie, you're late," said a little white bunny rabbit as he wiggled his pink nose. "Next time I have to wait, I'm walking up to the nearest human being and telling him the one about the duck who walked into the restaurant and—"

So much for cute. Sabrina said, "I'm sorry. I had to lug all this stuff from the pet store, and—"

"We ain't interested in your excuses," a raccoon informed her. "Just hand over the stuff and no one gets hurt."

Sabrina gulped. "I—I won't be late again."

"Hey, this is the discount brand," the bunny complained as he stuffed his little mouth with rabbit feed. "Next time get Bartlett's Best."

"But that costs twice as much," Sabrina protested.

"You get it, or we sing," the bunny warned her.

Sabrina sighed. "And I used to think you guys were cute," she said to the raccoon.

"Well, we used to think you were powerful," the raccoon retorted.

Sabrina itched to use her pointer finger on him. "Yeah, well, just wait until I can use my magic again. You'll be sorry."

"Huh." The raccoon chomped down another hefty mouthful. "I'll believe it when I see it."

"Oh, you'll see it all right," she muttered. "In fact, I plan to—"

The raccoon cleared its throat. Sabrina turned around.

Three men in sunglasses faced her. The tallest one said, "Pardon us, miss. We're conducting a field study in this part of the forest. Would you mind keeping your voice down?"

She swallowed nervously. "Of course."

The shortest one ticked his head toward her and flipped open a notebook. "Would you state your reason for mimicking the voices of various mammalian life-forms?"

"It's for a play," she said quickly. "It's about a girl with multiple personalities. She thinks she's all kinds of people including"—she took a quick inventory of the animals surrounding her—"a fox, a cat, a field mouse, a chipmunk, and a very greedy and picky bunny." She licked her lips, not sure how much the men had overheard. "The raccoon's actually the villain."

"Hey," the raccoon protested.

"See?" Sabrina asked in a high-pitched voice. "I did that!"

The spy guys looked at one another and shrugged. The one with the notebook jotted down a few things.

"Please continue on," he said. To the others, he gestured. "Let's move along. There's nothing here."

After they left the scene, the raccoon looked at Sabrina and said, "There's nothing here *yet.*"

Oh, dear.

Rattled, Sabrina hurried home. She charged upstairs and went through all her clothes, searching for spare change to buy more bribes with. But what good would that do? Sooner or later—probably sooner—she was going to run out of money for treats, and the animals would talk.

Just then the phone rang.

It was Valerie. "I have a huge, huge, huge favor to ask you. Could you walk Abdul this afternoon? Mom's taking us to see my grandparents. I'll give you the dollar."

A dollar would buy one-third of a chew bone. . . . Sabrina said, "Sure, Valerie, okay."

"He'll be in the Chesslers' side yard." Valerie sighed. "That way Libby doesn't have to bother talking to me."

Sabrina showed up promptly at 3:30. Sure enough, the big Irish setter was waiting. The first thing he said was, in a thick Irish accent, "Oh, begorah and bigosh, sure and I don't know what that Valerie's talking about. Those pants are actually quite flattering."

"What?" She blinked and looked down at her chocolate brown pants. They were her favorites.

"She told Ida Koljonen they make you look a wee bit *hippy,* was her word. I'll be saying now that I totally disagree."

Sabrina was stung. "What else has she been saying about me?" More to the point, she realized, was if she had been saying those things to Abdul. "Have you been talking around her?"

Abdul scratched behind his ear for fleas. "Can't say as I have, me girl. Haven't found much use for it, I must say."

Sabrina smiled at him. "I never thought Libby's dog would be so nice."

"In the Old Country we have a saying: You can't judge a dog by its owner. Now, if you don't mind, I sure would like a stretch of me legs."

"Of course."

Abdul pulled slightly on his leash as Sabrina opened the gate. Soon they were walking briskly down the street. Men in black suits skulked in the bushes and behind the trees, talking into all manner of strange objects. Sabrina kept peering back at her shadow, trying to see if the pants were indeed unflattering.

"Good day to you, Mistress Snowball," Abdul greeted a tortoiseshell cat sitting on a fence.

The cat looked up sleepily. "Sabrina," she said

in a friendly tone, "I'm sure you're eager to get to those Halloween presents."

"What?" Sabrina perked up.

"In the invisible closet in your bedroom? Your Aunt Zelda put them all in there."

"Snowball, whisst," Abdul remonstrated. "Witches like surprises for Halloween."

"Oops, sorry. Just pretend you didn't hear that," Snowball said merrily, and closed her eyes again.

Please, Sabrina thought. *Stop talking!*

They moved on. A Dalmatian trotted up to them. Sabrina recognized the spotted dog as Crystal, who lived next door to Harvey. Crystal said, "Heya, Sabby, I'll bet it really bothers you, knowing that Libby's at Harvey's studying while you're walking the Abster for a buck an hour."

"Excuse me? She's singing in a band," Sabrina said.

Crystal laughed. "Yeah, right. That lasted an hour. She had a big fight with Brian Enders and quit."

"Abdul, is this true?" Sabrina demanded.

The big red dog lowered his tail between his legs. "Oh, Sabrina, don't be asking me to tell tales on me mistress."

Harvey's studying with Libby. . . . Valerie is gossiping about my clothes to other girls. . . . Sabrina couldn't wait to put an end to talking with the animals. *On the other hand, it's . . .*

tempting . . . to know that there's a secret stash of Halloween presents for me, just waiting to be opened—

A man stepped from behind a bush and said into his wrist, "Apparently subject is just a girl walking a dog."

Sabrina swallowed. But not tempting enough. It was time to take much more drastic action.

Chapter 10

☆

☆

Sabrina took Abdul home. He thanked her for a lovely walk and assured her that Harvey was studying with Libby only because he needed to pass his biology test on Thursday so that he could play in the upcoming game.

"If I weren't so busy, I could have helped him," Sabrina groused.

"That's as it may be," Abdul said kindly. "But I wouldn't worry about it."

She walked home. One of Dr. Imperium's spy vans inched slowly down her street. Six government guys were trampling Aunt Hilda's daisies in the front yard.

And to cap it all off, Salem was asleep in her closet on her favorite sweater. She sighed and started to pick him up when he made a horrible retching noise.

"Sorry," he said, coming to groggily. "Hair ball."

"That's it!" Sabrina cried, dropping him. "I'll throw the animals a Hair Ball. No, a Fur Ball. And I'll get all the furry people to come, and then I'll explain what's going on so they stop talking, and I'll make sure they have a really good time, and—"

Salem rolled on his back and yawned. "Sorry, Sabrina. You lost me back there when you announced you had a hair ball."

She shook her head. "No. I'm going to give one."

"I don't want one," the cat replied.

"Oh, Salem," she said, laughing, and raced out of the room.

"Oh, *Salem?*" he replied. "I'm not the one who's not making any sense." He flopped over on his side.

"And get off my sweater," she called back to him.

He frowned. "How does she always *know?*"

Sabrina raced down into the basement and found the boxes filled with the paper plates and party decorations from her Halloween party last year. Then she opened up the box labeled HILDA'S RECORD COLLECTION and discovered that packed away with all the old records was an old-fashioned record player, the kind they had before CDs. It seemed a needle actually cut into the surface of the record to make it play.

"Amazing. What will they think of next?" she murmured. She opened more boxes and found all kinds of neat stuff. *This is going to be great!*

But how do you secretively cart all the decorations, kibble, records, and record player to the middle of the forest *and* spread the word about the Fur Ball in one short day?

The next afternoon Sabrina offered to walk Abdul for Valerie again, who was glad to be rid of the task. She told him her dilemma, and at first he suggested she wait a couple of days to hold the party. That way she'd have more time to organize it and get the word out.

"Um, I don't have more time," she said, feeling guilty. After all, she was doing all this so she could silence the animals.

"Oh, of course. Because of the full moon and all," Abdul observed.

"Oh." She swallowed. "You know?"

"About Castanalia and the Quizmaster and all the rest? And I'm sure that I do." He swiveled his head and winked at her. "As I recall, a little leprechaun told me the entire story."

"Salem," Sabrina gritted.

"Oh, no, no, 'twas a real leprechaun, sure as I'm a talking dog."

"There are leprechauns in Westbridge? Cool!"

Abdul gave a little tug on his leash. "Take me to that phone pole, please. It's got me name on it." He chuckled. "Now we each know a secret.

You know about the little people, and I know you must take away me voice."

"I'm very sorry," she said sincerely. She led him over to the phone pole and discreetly turned her head.

"Oh, whisha, whisha, don't worry yourself. I've thought about it, and I know it's for the best, really. If one of them government boyos catches us speaking, they'll ship us off to their research laboratories, and we'll never know a moment's peace again. Nor will this town. Westbridge will end up on *Sightings* for certain."

"Do you know if any of the others feel this way?"

"Aye, they do. Many of them. But I'm thinking *you* should explain it at the party."

"Okay. Then we need to get busy." She got an idea. "I'll ask everyone to carry something to the forest, and meanwhile you try to tell as many animals as you—"

Abdul cleared his throat. "Whsst," he warned.

She looked up to see Vice-principal Kraft standing practically nose to nose with her. At the end of a rhinestone leash stood a very tiny dachshund.

"Good afternoon, Mr. Kraft," Sabrina said cheerily.

Mr. Kraft looked from Sabrina to Abdul and back again. "What on earth are you doing? Talking to your dog?"

Uh-oh. She grimaced as she tried to think

something up. "It's Libby's dog," she blurted. Then she added. "Practicing for a play? Yes! It's called *One Hundred and One Irish Setters*. It's an adaptation." She squirmed.

At that moment a government guy strode around them. He was talking into a shoe. He gestured to a man perched on a telephone pole across the street.

Mr. Kraft's dog grinned up at Sabrina. Then it actually winked. Sabrina got even more nervous.

"It's, um, a very funny play," she said quickly.

Mr. Kraft eyed her. "Something's up with you, Miss Spellman. And someday I'm going to find out what it is."

Abdul and the dachshund were rubbing noses and making little barking noises at each other.

"Yes, sir. I mean, no, sir, nothing's up with me." Her voice was squeaky. "I'm just a regular kid."

"Mmm-hmm. Well, enjoy your walk with your dog." He tugged on his leash. "Heel, Lisa Marie."

Despite the situation, Sabrina hid a smile as she remembered Elvis's appearance at West-bridge High and how delighted Mr. Kraft had been to meet him. The vice-principal had even named his dog after Elvis's daughter!

Abdul murmured, "She'll help us."

Mr. Kraft cocked his head. "Did you say something, Miss Spellman?"

Sabrina jumped, startled. "Yes, yes, I did actually. Um, I asked you what time it was."

"It's four o'clock," he said without looking at his watch. "I walk Lisa Marie every day at precisely the same time. In fact, Lisa Marie is due at the vet's in twenty minutes."

"Oh, no, not the vet!" the little dog yipped.

Sabrina made her mouth very tiny and yipped, "I just hate the vet!"

Mr. Kraft frowned at her. "That's not very amusing."

"Sorry. Well, we'd better get going." She cleared her throat and Abdul loped on.

As soon as they were out of earshot, she said, "That was close." And it was getting closer all the time. The animals were becoming so used to talking that they were forgetting to be careful about it.

"I told her about the Fur Ball," Abdul said. "She's going to let all her friends know about it."

"Good." She sighed, wishing she could let her fingers do the conjuring. It was hard to believe there'd been a time she'd been upset that she had magical powers.

Sabrina spent the rest of the day preparing for the Fur Ball. Enlisting the aid of one of history's great strategists—none other than Salem—she met the animals in twos and threes in the basement. They unpacked the boxes of party favors and loaded them into tiny harnesses and wagons strapped to the backs of chipmunks, rats, raccoons, and the few cats who were not too lazy to pitch in. Since there was a leash law in Westbridge, they left the dogs out of their plan.

Then the animals dodged every single G-man and scientist as they made their way to the rendezvous point in the woods. In the darkening afternoon Sabrina strung the garlands of pumpkins and skeletons between the branches of the trees. She prepared a punch bowl of water and piled a picnic blanket with paper plates brimming with kibble, Pretty Kitty cat food, pieces of cheese, crackers, and table scraps. The box labeled YE OLDE PARTY FAVORS, 1603 yielded some dried animal knucklebones. Salem explained that in the olden days, people used knucklebones for dice. She decided to put them in goody bags for the dogs.

In the basement she found an old gasoline generator that she decided to use to supply electricity to the record player. Life before portable boom boxes sure was complicated! Then she set it up on a tree stump. Salem hopped up beside it, humming as he pawed through the records. He had offered to be the disc jockey.

By the light of the nearly full moon Sabrina waited for her guests to show up.

A wolf howled. A dog bayed.

A cat screeched, "It's party time!"

The dogs and cats began showing up, and then a pack of mice, and then a family of foxes.

Sabrina was delighted to see Lisa Marie, Mr. Kraft's dog, who informed her that Yes, Mr. Kraft actually had a black velvet painting of Elvis in his living room.

"Let's start the fun," Salem said. "Here's a little number by that swingin' cat, Hairy Belafonte."

The animals swarmed over the party food and began to dance. Sabrina watched anxiously for spy-types. Surely they would hear all the ruckus.

"Oh, Sabrina!" one of the mice squeaked. "We're just having the best best best time!"

"Yes, we are!" Crystal agreed. "This is the nicest thing a person's ever done for us."

Sabrina took that as her cue. Salem cut the music, and Sabrina stood up on the stump. "Well, I hope that you'll do something nice for me in return," she began. Abdul encouraged her with a quick nod. "I gathered you all here tonight to ask you—beg you—not to talk anymore until we can get Dr. Imperium out of town." She took a breath and went on. "If he hears even one peep—so to speak—out of any of you, he will never, ever leave us in peace. You'll all be shipped off to Washington for experiments, and we'll probably be on every talk show in the known universe."

"Typical," Salem drawled under his breath. "We get all the grief and you get all the glory."

"It won't be glory," Sabrina insisted. "It will be misery. No one will have a normal life again."

One of the mice said, "But what will happen to us when he leaves leaves leaves? You'll change us back, won't you? We'll go back to being dumb dumb dumb animals."

"Thank heaven," Salem muttered as the animals began to grumble. "I'm getting nowhere with this group as it is. All they care about are their walks and their Pretty Kitty."

Sabrina clapped her hands. "Listen! If you help me get rid of Dr. Imperium, I promise that on every Castanalia, my first spell will be to allow you to talk for the entire day and night. That way you won't have to hide it, and you can say anything you want to anybody."

"That's kind of neat," Crystal the dog said.

"I'd love to be able to tell off old Kraft," Lisa Marie added. "Everything is just too organized for my taste. We go on the same route every day. I eat the same thing every night. You can set your watch to my life." She groaned. "Except for going to the vet. Shots," she explained.

Salem said, "Well, at least you didn't get—"

"Well, I'm thinking this is a good compromise," Abdul volunteered, steering the discussion away from the delicate matter of vets. "It was kind of Sabrina to give us voices in the first place. We can return a favor with a favor, and still come out ahead."

"So, all in favor of the sounds of silence, raise your hand. Er, your paw," Sabrina urged.

The clearing filled with upraised paws, claws, and jaws.

"Good. Problem solved!" Sabrina cheered.

"Don't count your chickens," Salem intoned in a solemn whisper. "We may have won the battle, but we haven't won the war yet."

"I'll bet you my favorite sweater Dr. Imperium's out of here by tomorrow afternoon," Sabrina said smugly.

"You're on." Salem licked his forepaw. "And you'd better hope you're right. Tomorrow night's the full moon. And if these clowns can still talk, I'm moving."

It took a long time to clean up after the party, and Sabrina was exhausted. But as she led the first group of animals back to the house to put away the records and record player, she heard wild laughter coming from her living room.

She entered, to find Hilda and Zelda laughing hysterically on the couch.

"Aunt Hilda, Aunt Zelda! What's going on?"

"Dr. Imperium proposed to Zelda," Hilda said. She wiped her eyes and chuckled some more. "Thank goodness you came in, dear. We might have actually laughed ourselves to death. It's happened to witches, you know."

Zelda nodded, as she, too, calmed down. "But it's a nice way to go."

Sabrina stood before them. Zelda looked at

Hilda, and they started to burst out again, but at a look from Sabrina, they both fought it down.

"Actually, this is very bad news," Zelda said. "He told me he's going to stay in Westbridge as long as it takes to get me to say yes."

"But then the Witches' Council will keep the ban on magic use in place. And I have to reverse my spell by tomorrow night!" Sabrina cried.

"I know, dear." Zelda frowned. "Somehow, we're going to have to make him leave."

Sabrina slumped. Talk about losing the war.

Just then Salem sauntered in wearing a "Happy Halloween" party hat with a noisemaker in his mouth. Sabrina looked at him and glumly said, "Get my sweater and start packing."

☆

Chapter 11

☆

The next morning there was a knock on Sabrina's front door. She opened it to find Harvey on the porch.

"Hi," he said. "I thought we could walk to school together. We haven't seen much of each other all week."

"Yes," she said, pleased. She grabbed her bag and called goodbye to her aunts. They'd pulled an all-nighter thinking about Sabrina's dilemma, but were insistent she go to school and act as normal as possible. "I guess you've been studying a lot after school?"

"Yeah. With Libby."

"How nice of her," Sabrina deadpanned.

"Yeah." Harvey waved at one of the guys on Sabrina's lawn. "Morning!" To Sabrina's surprise, the man in black smiled and waved back at

Harvey. Harvey was like that, a likable, friendly person who never thought ill of anyone. Including Libby.

"All ready for tonight's game?" Harvey asked.

And the Harvest Dance? Sabrina wanted to add. He hadn't asked her to go. As far as she knew, he hadn't asked Libby, either. It was funny, but now that she had bigger things to worry about, the dance seemed fairly unimportant.

But not *totally* unimportant.

"Sure. I'm ready," she told him. "Are you going to start?"

"Coach is still working on the lineup," Harvey admitted. "I'm a nervous wreck. All I've been able to think about is tonight."

"I know just how you feel," Sabrina said sincerely as they crossed the street to Westbridge High.

"Hey, Kinkle. Heads up!" someone shouted. A football came flying at them. Harvey ran ahead to catch it.

Just then Snowball poked her head out of the bushes. "Hi, Sabrina. Cool party."

"Yeah! It was swell!" Artie the chipmunk enthused from an overhanging tree branch.

"Shhh! You guys *promised* not to talk," Sabrina said through clenched teeth. On the entrance to the school steps Mr. Kraft stood with his arms folded as the students filed into the

building. She couldn't let him see her talking to any animals.

Then inspiration struck. She said to the chipmunk and the cat, "Meet me at lunch, okay? I've got a plan."

"Gotcha." Snowball disappeared back into the bushes.

"It's a date, doll." Artie skittered back across the tree branch.

Harvey trotted back to her with a football under his arm. "Hey, you look happy."

"I'm that way," Sabrina answered breezily. Then she took a deep breath. "Hey, um, Harvey, are you going to the Harvest Dance?"

He looked confused. "Of course I am. I thought I was going with you. Libby said she passed the word for me. I've been so busy with practice, and your phone's been tied up."

Salem, she thought, *and Libby. Great!* "I guess she forgot. Well, that's . . . great. I'll, um, figure out what to wear." If all went well, she'd be able to point herself into something that would knock his socks off.

If all didn't, she doubted there would even be a dance.

"Hi!" Valerie joined them at her locker. "What's new?"

"Oh, nothing much," Sabrina said lightly. The bell rang. "We'd better go have a nice, normal day," she suggested, and led the way to home-room.

All day long Sabrina watched the clock. At lunch she discussed her plan with Snowball and Artie, and they agreed to spread the word. Then she called her aunts and clued them in.

"I don't know, Sabrina. It's so risky," Zelda said.

"I can't think of anything else to do," Sabrina told her. "Can you?"

Zelda thought a moment. "No, dear, I can't. We'll help you in every way we can."

"All right."

Sabrina went to the cafeteria and joined Valerie and Harvey. She said, "Val, I'll walk Abdul for you again today."

"Oh, I can't let you do that," Valerie said. "You've done it all week."

"You have to let me," Sabrina said urgently. "I mean, I really enjoy it. In fact, I'm thinking of starting a dog-walking service."

"Well . . ." Valerie sighed. "I was going to tell Libby that I quit. It hasn't gotten me anywhere socially. Some surprise."

"Okay, well, I'll walk him one more time. And then you can quit." Sabrina was sorry for Abdul. He really seemed to enjoy getting out and away from Libby. Maybe they could work out another arrangement.

* * *

The day dragged by. Then finally it was time to pick up Abdul.

"Sure and I almost had bad news for you," the Irish setter told her as they headed off. "Seems Mr. Kraft thought of revising his schedule, on account of the football game. But Lisa Marie looked up at him so very sadly, and he's had a change of heart."

"Whew. Thank goodness," Sabrina said.

"Me thinking as well," the setter replied.

Meanwhile, in the Spellman living room, Zelda took a deep breath, smiled at Dr. Imperium—whom she had invited over for tea again, and who was practically drooling on her antique toss pillow—and said, "Francisco, I was wondering if we might take a walk?"

"Whatever your heart desires, my pet," he replied, smiling brilliantly at her and offering her his arm.

"Have fun," Hilda called after them.

As they headed out the door, Zelda glanced at her watch. It was 3:50. She sped up her pace, and the scientist matched it.

As usual, the unsmiling government agents were milling up and down the street. Zelda said sweetly, "So tell me, Francisco. Have you found any evidence of witchcraft in Westbridge?"

He sighed. "No. But I'm hopeful." He smiled at her. "In more ways than one."

Zelda sighed. She didn't like tricking him, but there seemed to be no other way to get him out of town.

"In fact," he confided, "I've sent in a preliminary report that, ah, emphasizes my hopefulness. Overemphasizes it, actually."

"You mean, you lied?" she asked, somewhat shocked.

"Well, I wouldn't say *lied*, exactly. *Exaggerated* may be a better word."

"Which means the same thing," she observed.

Out of the corner of her eye she noticed one of the agents watching the two of them very closely. He pressed something against his ear and spoke into his suit cuff.

At the end of the block the door to Dr. Imperium's van slid open, and Colonel Van De Ven stood in the doorway, looking very unhappy.

She glanced down at her watch. It was 3:55.

"We'd better hurry," she said. "Ah, I have to be home soon to help Sabrina get ready for the big football game."

"They're on their way," Abdul told Sabrina. "I can smell them."

Salem led the troops. Soon about two dozen cats, dogs, mice, rats, and raccoons traveled from all over Westbridge toward the appointed rendezvous spot: the telephone pole with Abdul's name written all over it.

"I hope this works," Sabrina murmured.

"Sabrina, me girl, don't be nervous," Abdul told her.

"Oh, I'm not," she assured him.

He chuckled. "I can smell your fear." He slowed down. "Target within range," he reported. "Mr. Kraft is coming down the street."

"You can smell him?"

"Oh, yes. And his little dog, too." He took another sniff. "And your lovely auntie and that awful man."

Sabrina looked across the street. There were her aunt and Dr. Imperium. She gave a wave, and Zelda waved back.

"Fancy meeting you here," Sabrina said. "I was just saying to . . . *myself,*" she said, catching herself "what a nice day for a walk it is."

"Absolutely," Dr. Imperium said, his teeth chattering. Sabrina realized for the first time that it was a bit blustery. She'd been so nervous she hadn't even noticed.

Just then Mr. Kraft wheeled around the corner in a heavy coat and Lisa Marie on her leash. Sabrina caught her breath.

All at once Salem's troops bounded toward the vice-principal. In a chorus they started calling to him.

"Willard!"

"Hey, V.P.!"

"Fearless Leader!"

"Our master!"

Sabrina made a great show of coming to a dead stop as Abdul raced forward and bounded up to Mr. Kraft. He planted his front paws on Mr. Kraft's chest. Then he began to lick Mr. Kraft's face, saying, "He gave us our voices! He's our special witch pal!"

"Oh, my heavens!" Dr. Imperium shouted.

Zelda clapped her hands together. "Francisco, I'm so terrified!" she cried. "What's happening?"

"Witchcraft!" Dr. Imperium exulted. "At last!"

"What's the meaning of this?" Mr. Kraft shouted as the animals gathered around him.

Suddenly the street was packed with government agents. At least six of them waved magicometers in Mr. Kraft's direction. Cameras flashed. Other agents started gathering up the animals, including Abdul, who gave Sabrina the doggy equivalent of a thumbs-up.

Then the van screeched up to the curb, and two agents hustled Mr. Kraft toward it.

"Stop! What are you doing? I'm an American citizen! I have rights! You can't do this!" Mr. Kraft shouted.

"Be silent, witch!" Dr. Imperium said, shaking his fist. He clasped both Zelda's hands in his. "My darling, I must attend to this."

"Oh, Francisco, be careful," Zelda pleaded. "After all, this is *magic.*"

"I will. I have a special antimagic vest," he confided. "I've been wearing it all week." He leaned toward her, then dared to kiss her on the cheek. "I'm going to be so famous," he crowed. Then he dashed into the van.

"Hoo, boy," Sabrina said to her aunt. "You almost want to warn him, know what I mean?"

Salem came up beside her. "No, I do not."

"Your troops have been briefed, right?" Sabrina asked him.

"They know exactly what to do," Salem answered proudly.

The three stood for a moment as the van pulled away. Then Zelda let out a little sigh. "Let's go home. Hilda will be dying to find out how it went."

Sabrina eagerly led the way.

☆

Chapter 12

☆

Hilda greeted them at the door with a chocolate-chip cookie in each hand.

"I think it's going to work," Sabrina told her as she and Zelda took the cookies. "These are great. Did you actually bake them?"

"I know it's going to work," Hilda said. "Come with me and see for yourself. And, no, I didn't actually bake them, but I did actually purchase them at the actual grocery store."

"Aunt Hilda, get down with your bad self," Sabrina teased her.

Hilda took them into the living room and flicked the TV on with the remote. The national news was on with their favorite anchor, Toni Ballo. She was their favorite because it was a hoot to say, "Live at five with Toni Baloney."

"This just in. In Westbridge, Massachusetts,

Dr. Francisco Imperium has called a press conference in one hour to present positive proof of the existence of witchcraft."

"An hour," Sabrina fretted. "What's he waiting for?"

"The senator's plane," Salem said as he came into the room. "Mmm, I smell some chocolate chips with my name on them."

"Senator? Which senator?" Sabrina asked.

Salem looked around. "Where are the cookies? I'm starving. Ah." He jumped onto the couch and from there, onto the coffee table, where a plate of cookies was laid out. "Yum." He scarfed one and then another. "None other than Mr. Richard David Wilkinson, one of our men in Washington."

Sabrina said, "Really? How'd he contact him so fast?"

"It seems the senator is the one who okayed his funding for this fabulous witchcraft project. Now he's flying in to take the credit." Salem burped. "You'd know all this stuff, too, if you'd just bribe some mice to eavesdrop on all incoming and outgoing phone calls."

Sabrina looked at Hilda and Zelda with a raised eyebrow, then back at the cat. "And the animals know what to do, right? No one's going to flub."

"Sabrina, my minions are trained professionals." Salem took another cookie. "These are terrific. Much better than the ones you ladies conjure up."

"Gee, thanks." Sabrina was miffed. Two years of home ec, and what did she have to show for it?

"Well, I guess we'll have to sit tight for the press conference," Hilda said. She headed for the kitchen. "I bought each of you your own half-gallon of ice cream. Except Salem. He gets frozen yogurt." She smiled at him. "Because of your diet."

"Unfair," he wailed.

"You can have some of mine," Sabrina whispered to him. "I owe you." Even if he did prefer store-bought cookies over hers.

"You're a doll. I'll try not to claw your sweater."

They ate all the ice cream and then moved on to microwave popcorn. Sabrina was beginning to feel a little ill, and to actually crave something good for her, when Toni Baloney broke into their *Brady Bunch* rerun and said, "Dr. Francisco Imperium is waiting live from the sleepy little town of Westbridge, where he has a startling announcement. Our roving reporter, April Khabazian, is standing by. April?"

The screen filled with the head and shoulders of a woman with fluffy blond hair. Then the camera pulled back to reveal her standing in front of Dr. Imperium's van.

"Toni, the air is crackling with excitement

here in Westbridge," she said through her nose. "It seems that Dr. Francisco Imperium, a noted researcher based at the Pentagon itself, has made a startling discovery. I'm told that he will be joining us shortly, and—"

The van door opened. Dr. Imperium stood in the doorway, Mr. Kraft at his side. The vice-principal looked dazed and confused.

Around them, Salem's troops swarmed and hopped out of the van. Instantly they were surrounded by government agents in dark glasses. Sabrina saw Abdul, Lisa Marie, and many of her other newfound friends. She hoped they remembered what they were supposed to do . . . or rather, to not do.

The camera zoomed in on Dr. Imperium. "Greetings," he said, raising his hand. "I am Dr. Francisco Imperium, and I have something to reveal to the world. I have concrete proof of the existence of witchcraft."

Just then another man appeared in the van doorway. It was the senator, who was smiling broadly.

"I'll bet you five dollars his teeth were also actually purchased," Hilda said. No one took her up on her bet.

"This is Senator Wilkinson, who sponsored my research," Dr. Imperium continued. "He has seen for himself what I'm about to show all of you out there in TV land!"

"Who writes his stuff?" Hilda said.

Zelda sighed. "He's got a good heart."

"I'm sure they said the same thing about Attila the Hun," Salem retorted.

"Actually, they didn't," Zelda said. "And he didn't have a good heart."

Dr. Imperium pointed at Mr. Kraft. "Go," he said.

Mr. Kraft looked left, right, then straight at the camera. He said, "I have no idea how this happened to me," and pointed at the animals.

Nothing did happen, to him or the animals.

He pointed again.

Dr. Imperium gestured impatiently to the silent creatures. "Speak! Speak!" he urged.

They all stared at him. Then they began to mill around, as animals do. The raccoon started searching the pockets of the nearest government guy, and the mice disappeared under the van.

"Mr. Kraft," Dr. Imperium urged. "Use your magic." He looked into the camera. "Willard Kraft is a warlock, you see. We helped him discover his gifts with our advanced scientific equipment."

Mr. Kraft clumsily waved his hands at the remaining animals. They completely ignored him.

"Francisco?" the senator said, softly, menacingly.

"Wait. Perhaps there's some interference affecting Mr. Kraft's performance. It may be low-level magnetic radiation from our equipment, or the hole in the ozone layer. Yes." He pulled a notebook from his pocket. "Or—"

"Or it could be a hoax," Colonel Van De Ven said from the doorway to the van. He stepped down and walked over to April Khabazian. He was carrying a small boom box. "Listen to this." He pressed a button. And everyone listening to the national news heard:

"Have you found any evidence of witchcraft in Westbridge?" That was Aunt Zelda's voice!

On the tape, Dr. Imperium answered, *"No. But I'm hopeful. In more ways than one. In fact, I've sent in a preliminary report that, ah, emphasizes my hopefulness. Overemphasizes it, actually."*

"You mean, you lied?"

"Well, I wouldn't say lied, *exactly.* Exaggerated *may be a better word."*

"Which means the same thing."

Colonel Van De Ven clicked off the recorder. "'Which means the same thing.'" He turned to the senator. "Sir, my deepest apologies, and my assurances that the military had nothing to do with this."

"Dr. Imperium." The senator's face glowed a dark purple. "Your explanation, please?"

"But, but . . ." The man stared at Mr. Kraft. "Do something!"

"I will," Mr. Kraft said, stomping out of the picture. "I'll sue you for harassment!"

"Stop the cameras!" the senator shouted. "I will not be a party to this insanity."

Suddenly someone wrestled the camera to the ground. The picture whirled and then everything went black.

Toni Baloney looked shaken. She said, "More, after these commercials."

The phone rang. Zelda put it on the speaker phone and then answered it.

"Zelda, my darling. It's Francisco." His voice shook. "The senator is closing down my operation. My entire staff and I have fifteen minutes to leave town."

"Yes!" Sabrina squealed, high-fiving Aunt Hilda. Then she lowered her voice and whispered, "Way to go, Salem."

"Oh, dear," Zelda murmured sympathetically. "I'm so sorry."

"I can't figure out what went wrong. Those animals did talk! But there also seems to be several reports of your niece practicing animal voices for a play."

"Yes, a play," Zelda confirmed. "It's supposed to be very good."

"How could I have blundered so?" He sighed heavily. "Zelda, I must go back to Washington and analyze all my data to see where I went wrong. That is, if I have any funding left to do any analysis. I can't ask you to go with me, dearest. Not when I'm disgraced like this."

"Oh, alas, Francisco," Zelda said mournfully.

"Don't try to talk me out of it. Someday, if I can vindicate myself, I will come back for you. But, Zelda . . ." He exhaled. "Don't wait forever."

"Francisco . . ."

"I have to hang up. The van's leaving. Farewell."

"Farewell."

Zelda hung up. For a moment she lowered her head, and then she burst into a fit of giggles. "That poor man!" she said, laughing.

In the kitchen the toaster popped.

"Memo," Salem said, "from the Other Realm."

Uh-oh. Sabrina led the race into the kitchen. She pulled the memo from the toaster and read:

> *To: All magic users, including leprechauns*
> *Subject: Magic ban*
> *Due to the extreme ineptitude of the mortal scientist Dr. Francisco Imperium, the ban on magic use is hereby revoked.*
> *Having been apprised of the situation concerning Ms. Sabrina Spellman and her One Thing, the Witches' Council has determined that she shall perform one thousand hours of community service in the Other Realm as punishment.*

"One thousand hours?" Sabrina wailed.

"One thousand hours?" Salem grumbled. "And *I* was turned into a *cat* for *less?*"

"Salem, I'd quit while I was behind if I were you," Hilda said. "Did you guys know we had leprechauns in Westbridge?"

Zelda smiled at Sabrina. "Well, it's over. Just like Castanalia. Tell me, Sabrina, if you could cast any spell you wanted right now, what would it be?"

"I'd get out of the community service," Salem suggested.

Poof! The Quizmaster appeared and said, "That wish is granted!"

"Yay!" Sabrina cheered. "Really and truly?"

"Yes." He preened. "I told the council I didn't think it was fair, especially after you managed to discredit Dr. Imperium and solve your problem without resorting to magic, you deserved a reprieve."

"Whoo-hoo!"

He smiled at her aunts. "So much for council bureaucracy, eh, ladies?"

"You were eavesdropping!" Hilda cried.

"Maybe, maybe not." He shrugged and disappeared.

Then the doorbell rang. As Sabrina went to get it, her jeans and sweater magically transformed into the same beautiful white formal she had worn at the nonexistent rock concert/football game. A corsage of tiny white roses encircled her right wrist.

"Thanks, guys," she said happily as she opened the door.

There stood Harvey. His eyes widened and he said, "Wow, Sabrina, is that what you're going to wear to the dance?"

"Yes." She smiled at him. "I was just trying it on for size."

"Well, it looks great," he said amiably.

Suddenly Abdul hopped onto the porch and peeked from behind Harvey. Sabrina mouthed the words, "Next year."

Abdul nodded.

Sabrina pointed.

Abdul turned and silently trotted into the darkness. Sabrina felt a pang. She would miss their chats.

Harvey, who had not noticed the dog, said, "Hey, did you guys hear about that nutty scientist? He thought Mr. Kraft was a warlock!"

"Imagine that." Sabrina laced her arm through his. "You can't really blame him, though. Sometimes it seems as if there's magic in the air. Do you know what I mean?"

"Sure I do." Harvey smiled at her. "Like we'll make that first down even with me starting."

"Exactly." Sabrina turned to grin at her aunts. Hilda and Zelda both gave her victory signs.

Sabrina walked onto the porch with Harvey. The street was cluttered with vans and cars with darkened windows winding their way out of the little town of Westbridge.

"Well, that's probably the weirdest thing that's ever happened around here," Harvey said, gesturing to the line of traffic.

"Yup," Sabrina said. Except for the arrival of Elvis, and Valerie being a rock star, and Hilda being the President of the United States. And the food war and the musical revue with Deep-Freeze Chicky, and facials on Venus and—

And she could go on and on and on.

"Most definitely the weirdest," she agreed. She could hardly keep from giggling out loud.

And she could hardly wait for the next Castanalia. With all that time to plan her spells, "weird" wasn't even going to begin to describe the time she and her aunts were going to have!

About the Author

NANCY HOLDER lives in San Diego (exactly ninety-three miles south of Disneyland) with her husband, Wayne, their two-year-old daughter, Belle, Nancy's sister, Leslie, and everybody's three dogs, who are Mr. Ron, Maggie, and Dot. Wayne and Nancy share an office on the second floor of their house. They both consider themselves very lucky to work at home so they can play with Belle whenever they want. And Leslie, the resident neat freak, keeps them from drowning under the gobs of books, magazines, floppy disks, and toys they leave all over the place.

A four-time Bram Stoker award-winner for her work in supernatural fiction, Nancy has sold twenty-seven novels, including *Buffy the Vampire Slayer* books with her coauthor, Christopher Golden. She has also sold approximately two hundred short stories and Japanese comic books and TV commercials. She started writing in the second grade and hasn't stopped yet!